Book Three of The Taravale Series

EMILY FRASER

WHAT THE LAND REVEALS

What the Land Reveals

Book Three of The Taravale Series

First edition 2026

Published by Southern Ground Press, Australia

ISBN (paperback): 978-1-7645031-3-6

ISBN (ebook): 978-1-7645031-4-3

Printed in Australia

AUTHOR'S NOTE

What the Land Reveals is a story about absence.

Not just what goes missing - but what is deliberately erased. The people who aren't looked for. The questions that aren't asked. The way silence, when practiced long enough, begins to feel like truth.

Taravale is fictional. Its patterns are not.

This book sits at the point where pressure becomes danger, where restraint is no longer protection, and where love stops being careful. It is about what happens when the land itself contradicts the story it has been told to keep.

Some truths surface quietly. Others demand to be found.

Thank you for continuing the journey with Alice and Tom. The reckoning does not end here.

CHAPTER ONE

The puppy slept through the knock.

That, Alice would remember later - the way something so small and warm and alive had been completely untroubled by the sound that changed the direction of everything.

She didn't hear the knock at first either.

She was at the sink, hands in water, staring out at the paddock without really seeing it. Morning light lay across the land in pale bands, dust already lifting where the grass had thinned. The kind of morning that pretended it was ordinary.

The knock came again. Firmer this time.

Alice dried her hands on a tea towel and crossed the kitchen, the boards cool under her bare feet. She didn't feel uneasy - not yet. Just alert in the way you became when someone arrived without warning.

When she opened the door, the woman standing on the verandah looked like she had driven a long way without stopping.

Mid-thirties. Tired eyes. Hair pulled back with more force than care. A canvas bag slung over one shoulder, knuckles white where she gripped the strap.

"Are you Alice Gordon?" the woman asked.

"Yes."

The woman let out a breath that sounded like relief and dread tangled together. "My name's Claire Bennett. I'm sorry to just turn up. I didn't know who else to ask."

Alice stepped aside. "You'd better come in."

The puppy woke then - a soft huff of breath, a stretch, oversized paws sliding across the floor. He sat up, ears folding in on themselves, tail thumping once against the leg of the table.

Claire froze.

"Oh," she said quietly.

Alice glanced down. "He's new."

Claire nodded absently, eyes fixed on the dog like she was anchoring herself to something real. "He looks safe."

The word landed heavier than it should have.

Alice closed the door and gestured toward the table. "Do you want tea?"

"Yes," Claire said immediately. Then, after a beat, "Please."

They sat opposite each other, steam curling between them. The puppy wandered over and flopped down at Alice's feet, chin on her boot.

Claire watched that too.

"My brother came back here three weeks ago," she said finally. "He rang me from town. Said he was staying one night."

Alice's spine went still.

"What's his name?"

"Daniel Bennett."

The name didn't spark recognition. That, too, felt wrong.

"He never rang again," Claire continued. "His phone goes straight to voicemail. His car hasn't moved. And when I ask around, people keep telling me the same thing."

Alice met her gaze. "That he moved on."

"Yes." Claire's mouth tightened. "They say it like it's nothing. Like he always does that."

"Does he?"

Claire shook her head. "No. He tells me where he's going. Even when he doesn't want to."

Alice thought of the man in the photographs. The letters. The notebook.

"What was he doing here?" she asked.

Claire hesitated, then reached into her bag. She pulled out a folded piece of paper and slid it across the table.

Alice unfolded it slowly.

A name she recognised immediately stared back at her.

The man from the photos.

"He said he'd found something," Claire said quietly. "Something that explained why things happened the way they did. He said if he didn't come back, I should talk to you."

The puppy stirred at Alice's feet, tail thumping again, utterly unconcerned.

Alice looked up.

Claire's eyes were bright now, fixed, terrified.

"He wouldn't just disappear," she said. "Not like this."

Alice folded the paper and set it down carefully.

"No," she said. "He wouldn't."

Outside, the land lay quiet, holding its shape, giving nothing away.

But Alice already knew - with a certainty that settled deep in her chest - that this time, silence wasn't what they were dealing with.

This time, something had been taken.

CHAPTER TWO

Tom arrived just before dusk.

Alice saw the ute before she heard it - a familiar shape cutting along the fence line, dust rising behind it in a way that felt both ordinary and loaded. She stood at the kitchen window longer than necessary, watching it approach, bracing for something she couldn't quite name.

He hadn't called.

That was deliberate.

The engine cut. The door opened. Tom stepped out, boots hitting gravel with the same unhurried certainty she remembered. He paused for a moment, scanning the paddocks, the house, the sky - not looking for permission, just orienting himself to a place that still claimed him whether he wanted it to or not.

She was on the verandah when he stopped, hands resting on the rail, watching dust settle around the tyres. For a moment, neither of them moved.

Then he opened the passenger door.

A black-and-tan Kelpie puppy, all legs and intent, with paws slightly too big for the body he hadn't finished growing into yet, launched out, landing badly, recovering with dignity, and immediately sitting as if this had all been very carefully planned.

His ears hadn't decided what they wanted to be - one tipping forward, the other folding back on itself - but his eyes were steady and unnervingly serious for something so young.

"You made good time," she said.

Tom nodded. "Didn't want to leave it late."

He sounded careful. Not distant - *measured*. The kind of tone people used when they knew timing mattered.

Her eyes dropped then, drawn by movement at his feet.

The puppy sat squarely beside him. He looked up at Alice like he'd already placed her somewhere important.

Tom followed her gaze. "I hope that's alright."

Alice crouched automatically, instinct overriding surprise. "Where did you—"

"Picked him up this morning," Tom said. "Didn't plan to. But—"

Ash leaned forward, pressed his nose into her palm, and exhaled.

Alice felt something in her chest give way.

He smelled like dust and sun and the faint, sharp sweetness of new beginnings. His body was warm, solid, his heartbeat quick beneath her hand.

"What's his name?" she asked softly.

Tom hesitated. "Ash."

She looked up at him. "Why?"

Tom's gaze drifted to the paddocks, the brittle grass, the long memory of fire that never fully left places like this. "Because things burn," he said. "And still come back."

Ash's tail thumped once, firm and deliberate, like the decision had been agreed upon already.

"He's young," Tom added, as if justifying himself now. "But he's steady. Didn't spook at the road. Didn't spook at noise. Watched everything."

Alice stood slowly. "You brought him here."

"Yes."

"Why?"

Tom met her eyes. The carefulness slipped just enough to show something raw underneath. "Because I didn't want to leave you with empty space."

The words landed heavier than she expected.

Alice looked down at Ash again, at the way he'd settled against her boots without being asked. "You didn't think to ask first."

Tom's mouth twitched. "I figured you'd say no if I did."

She laughed softly, surprised by it. "You'd be right."

They stood there for a moment - the house behind them, the land stretching out ahead, Ash a small, breathing bridge between past and future.

Tom cleared his throat. "I won't stay long."

Alice didn't answer immediately.

Instead, she stepped aside. "Come in."

Inside, the house reacted to him the way it always had - not with warmth, exactly, but recognition. The floorboard near the sink creaked in the same place it always did. The hallway caught his shadow and held it.

Ash explored cautiously, nose down, mapping the space with methodical intent. He stopped at the closed door at the end of the hall, sat, and stared at it.

Alice felt her skin prickle.

"He does that a lot," Tom said quietly. "Stops where things don't add up."

Alice crossed the room and knelt beside the puppy. "That room's empty," she said, more to herself than to him.

Ash didn't move.

Tom watched them, something unreadable in his expression. "You don't have to keep him."

Alice looked up sharply. "You already named him."

Tom smiled faintly. "Didn't mean I expected him to stay."

She rested her hand on Ash's back, feeling the steady warmth there. "You brought him because you knew he would."

Tom didn't argue.

Later, they stood on the verandah together, mugs cooling between their hands as the light faded from the paddocks. Ash lay at their feet, already behaving like he'd always belonged.

"You're not wrong, you know," Alice said.

"About what?"

"Empty space."

Tom's gaze stayed on the land. "I remember what it does to people."

Alice leaned her shoulder lightly against his. Not a declaration. Not a retreat. Just contact.

"You didn't have to come," she said.

Tom nodded. "I know."

"And you brought him anyway."

"Yes."

Ash shifted, pressing closer to Alice's leg, a small weight with outsized certainty.

Alice looked out across Taravale, the lines of it sharp and familiar and suddenly less lonely.

"Alright," she said quietly. "He can stay."

Tom exhaled like he'd been holding something back. "Good."

Ash thumped his tail once, satisfied.

The land watched.

And somewhere between dust and dusk, something settled into place - not safely, not easily, but *deliberately*.

CHAPTER THREE

By midmorning, Taravale had agreed on a version.

Not loudly. Not formally. Just enough that when Alice asked the same question twice, she got the same answer back - shaped slightly differently each time, but identical at the core.

He moved on.

She started at the shop.

Linda rang up her bread and milk without meeting her eyes. "Daniel Bennett?" she said, brow creasing as if searching memory. "Can't say I remember him clearly."

"You sold him fuel," Alice said. "Three weeks ago."

Linda blinked. "Did I?"

"You did," Alice said evenly. "He paid cash."

Linda's fingers stilled on the counter. "Lots of people do."

"But you remember them."

Linda swallowed. "I remember trouble."

"That wasn't the question."

Linda looked past her then, toward the door, as if hoping someone else might come in and interrupt. When no one did, she leaned closer.

"He was quiet," she said. "Didn't cause a fuss. Just passing through."

"How long?"

Linda shrugged. "A night. Maybe two."

Alice nodded. "Where did he stay?"

Linda's shoulders lifted, fell. "Didn't ask."

Alice paid and stepped outside into the glare.

One answer.

At the servo, Jack wasn't on shift. The boy behind the counter checked the system twice before shaking his head.

"No record," he said. "If he was here, it didn't flag."

Alice watched the boy carefully. "The pumps were down that day."

The boy's eyes flicked up. "How do you know that?"

"Because I filled up here," Alice said. "Cash only."

He hesitated, then shrugged. "Maybe the system reset."

"Maybe," Alice said, and left.

At the post office, the woman behind the counter smiled too brightly.

"Daniel Bennett?" she said. "Can't say I remember the name."

"He collected a parcel," Alice said. "Registered."

The woman's smile wavered. "A lot of people collect parcels."

"But not registered ones," Alice replied. "Those gct signed for."

The woman's gaze hardened. "People drift through here all the time."

That was the phrase again.

Drift.

By the time Alice returned home, Ash was asleep in a patch of sun on the kitchen floor, legs twitching, chasing something harmless in his dreams. Tom stood at the bench, phone in hand, jaw tight.

"They're all saying the same thing," Alice said.

Tom didn't look up. "Because they've been told to."

"By who?"

Tom finally met her eyes. "Someone who benefits from consistency."

She set her keys down slowly. "They can't all be lying."

"No," Tom agreed. "But they can all be repeating."

Alice leaned against the table, crossing her arms. "Linda remembered the fuel. Until I named it."

Tom's mouth tightened. "That's your first crack."

"And the post office," Alice continued. "Registered parcel. They don't forget those."

Tom nodded once. "Someone's tidied the edges."

Ash stirred and rolled onto his back, paws in the air, completely unbothered.

Alice stared down at him. "They're acting like he was forgettable."

Tom's voice was low. "That's the trick. If you can make someone feel insignificant, you don't have to explain their absence."

Alice felt something cold settle behind her ribs.

Claire came in from the hallway, drawn by the tone. "Did you find anything?"

Alice hesitated. Then: "I found agreement."

Claire frowned. "That's not good."

"No," Tom said. "It's organised."

Claire's face drained of colour. "You think someone's done this on purpose."

Alice reached for the kettle and stopped herself, hand hovering, then lowering again. She didn't need tea. She needed clarity.

"When did Daniel last speak to you?" Alice asked.

Claire thought. "The night he arrived. He said the town felt... careful. Like he was being watched without anyone actually watching."

Tom's eyes flicked to Alice.

"No one's watching," Alice said quietly. "They don't need to."

Claire swallowed. "He said he'd found proof. Not just about the man in the photos. About something else. Something that kept happening."

"What kind of proof?" Tom asked.

"He wouldn't say," Claire replied. "Just that the land showed things people tried to bury."

Alice closed her eyes briefly.

Outside, a car slowed as it passed the gate. Didn't stop. Didn't speed up either.

Just enough to be noticed.

When Alice looked again, it was already gone.

Inside, Ash lifted his head and barked once - sharp, surprised - then settled again, uneasy now.

Tom moved to the window, scanning the road.

"Alright," he said quietly. "We don't ask questions in town anymore."

Alice nodded. "We look where they don't want us looking."

Tom met her gaze, something fierce and protective surfacing. "And we don't do it alone."

Alice felt the weight of the morning settle into purpose.

Because this wasn't about curiosity anymore.

Someone had decided Daniel Bennett didn't matter.

And Alice was about to prove that decision wrong.

CHAPTER FOUR

The town didn't say anything at first.

That was always how it started - with politeness. With nods that arrived a fraction too late and conversations that softened around the edges the moment Alice entered a room.

Alice felt it most when she walked alone.

The street looked the same. The bakery window still fogged in the mornings. The noticeboard outside the hall still held the same curling flyers, staples rusting slowly through paper that had outlived its relevance. But something in the air had shifted, thin and tight, like breath being held.

Ash padded beside her, lead slack between them, head up, eyes alert. He stopped once, ears tipping forward, staring at nothing in particular.

"What is it?" Alice murmured.

Ash didn't bark. He just watched.

At the post office, the woman behind the counter slid the mail across without comment, eyes fixed somewhere just past Alice's shoulder. No smile. No question.

"Thanks," Alice said.

The woman nodded once and turned away.

Outside, a ute idled longer than necessary before pulling out into the street. Dust rose and hung in the air, refusing to settle.

Alice kept walking.

At the shop, Linda greeted her too brightly. "You settling back in alright?"

Alice met her gaze evenly. "I am."

Linda hesitated. "Good. We all just want things... calm."

Ash shifted closer to Alice's leg.

"I imagine you do," Alice replied.

She left without buying anything.

Further down the road, she stopped at the creek crossing. The water ran low and steady, the banks worn smooth by years of passage. It looked harmless enough. Always had.

Ash tugged toward the edge, nose down, scenting something old and faint. He whined once, frustrated, then sat abruptly, staring at the water like it had offended him.

Alice followed his gaze.

Nothing moved.

No disturbance. No sign.

Just the quiet insistence that something here did not want to be remembered.

A car passed behind her. Slow. Not stopping. Not hurrying.

Alice straightened.

She didn't turn around.

Later, back at the house, she stood at the sink and watched dust settle across the paddocks, thinking of the way silence worked in places like this - how it didn't announce itself. How it simply made room for itself until speaking felt like a disruption.

Ash lay at her feet, chin on his paws, eyes half-closed but tracking everything.

"Not yet," Alice whispered, though she wasn't sure who she was reassuring.

Outside, Taravale held its breath.

And somewhere beneath the politeness, the land waited to see who would blink first.

Ash didn't like the place.

Alice noticed it before Tom did - the way the puppy's pace slowed as they left the ute, the way his tail dropped from its usual confident line and hovered uncertainly behind him. He stayed close to her left leg, brushing against her calf as they walked, nose lifting and lowering like he was trying to decide which scent mattered most.

"You feel it too," Alice murmured.

Tom glanced back. "What?"

"Ash."

The puppy stopped abruptly, ears tipping forward, then flattened slightly as he stared toward the far shed.

Tom followed his gaze. The structure sat low against the slope, corrugated iron dulled by years of dust and sun. One door hung crooked on its hinges. The track leading to it was faint - not unused, just careful.

"Could be nothing," Tom said.

Ash let out a low sound. Not a growl. Not a bark.

Disapproval.

Alice felt her shoulders tighten. "He hasn't made a noise like that yet."

Tom crouched and rested a hand briefly on the pup's chest. "Alright," he said quietly. "We go slow."

They moved forward together, the land flattening beneath their boots. Ash stayed between them, body small but alert, head swinging left and right as if mapping something they couldn't see.

The shed door creaked when Tom pushed it open.

Ash froze.

Every muscle in the puppy's body went tight, weight shifting back, hackles lifting just enough to notice. He didn't bolt. Didn't bark.

He stared.

The smell hit Alice a second later - old oil, dust, something metallic that didn't belong to the land.

"Stay," Tom whispered, though he hadn't trained the word yet.

Ash didn't move anyway.

Inside, the shed was mostly empty. A workbench. Rusted tools. A mattress rolled tightly and shoved against the wall like someone hadn't meant to leave it behind.

Alice stepped in and Ash followed, close now, pressed against her shin.

"Someone slept here," she said.

Tom nodded. "Recently."

Ash's nose dropped to the dirt floor. He tracked a short line, then stopped abruptly near the back corner. Sat. Looked up at Alice.

"That's not random," Tom said.

Alice crouched beside the puppy, fingers resting lightly between his shoulders. The ground there was disturbed - not dug, just scuffed, like something had been dragged and then repositioned with care.

"Daniel stayed here," Alice said. "Not for long."

Alice didn't touch the mattress.

It wasn't the dirt that stopped her - it was the care. The way it had been positioned, as if someone had intended to come back. As if leaving it visible but contained was part of the agreement they'd made with themselves.

Ash edged closer, nose working hard now, tail no longer wagging. He sniffed the air once, then sneezed sharply and shook his head like he was trying to dislodge something unpleasant.

Tom noticed. "What is it?"

"Not fear," Alice said quietly. "Confusion."

Ash moved again, slower this time, tracing a careful arc around the mattress without touching it. He stopped at the far wall and sat - deliberate, upright - staring at a point just above the concrete floor.

Alice's chest tightened.

"That's the second time he's done that today," she said.

Tom crouched beside the pup. "Done what?"

"Stopped where things don't line up."

She stepped closer, crouching beside Ash. The wall looked ordinary enough - corrugated iron, rusted at the base where moisture crept in. But the dirt beneath it was compacted differently. Pressed flat, then disturbed again. Not digging. Not hiding.

Repositioning.

"He didn't stay long," Alice murmured.

Tom nodded. "Long enough to realise he shouldn't."

Ash shifted suddenly, pressing back against Alice's legs, eyes flicking to the doorway.

That was when she noticed it - not a sound exactly, but an absence. The shed had gone too still. The birds outside had quieted, the breeze no longer stirring the loose edge of tin above them.

Alice straightened slowly.

"You feel that?" she whispered.

Tom didn't answer immediately. His gaze had lifted to the doorway, his body subtly repositioning - not shielding her, but aligning himself between her and the open ground beyond.

"Yes," he said quietly. "We're not alone."

Ash let out a low, vibrating sound deep in his chest - warning without panic.

A sound came from outside - gravel shifting under weight.

Tom's head snapped up. "Did you hear that?"

Ash barked once. Sharp. Loud. Wrong.

Tom moved immediately, hand going to Alice's arm, pulling her back against the workbench.

"Out," Tom said quietly. "Now."

They didn't run. Running would announce fear.

They stepped out into the light together, Ash glued to Alice's leg, barking once more as they crossed the threshold.

Nothing moved.

The paddock lay still, grass stirring gently, no ute, no person, no obvious explanation.

Tom scanned the tree line. "Someone was here."

"Or just left," Alice said.

Ash whined softly, then turned and faced the shed again, body squared, small but stubborn.

Tom crouched and rested a hand on his neck. "Good boy," he said quietly. "Good."

Alice swallowed. "He knew before we did."

Tom looked at her then, expression hard. "Which means someone didn't want us here."

Ash leaned into Tom's touch, then shifted back toward Alice, placing himself between her and the open ground without being told.

They stood there for a moment longer, the quiet pressing in around them differently now - not empty, not peaceful.

Watched.

"Alright," Tom said finally. "We've seen enough."

As they walked back toward the ute, Ash kept glancing over his shoulder, ears tipped back, tracking something only he could sense.

Alice rested a hand on his back, steadying both of them.

This wasn't curiosity anymore.

Someone had chosen this place because they thought no one would look.

And Ash had just proved that the land still noticed who passed through it.

CHAPTER SIX

The creek had always pretended to be harmless.

It slipped through the property narrow and clear most of the year, its banks worn smooth by cattle hooves and childhood crossings alike. Alice remembered it as a place of dares and warnings that were never properly explained - adults calling out half-hearted cautions from the fence line, never raising their voices enough to make a point.

Careful.
Not too far downstream.

No one ever said why.

Standing beside it now, Alice understood the omission wasn't forgetfulness. It was choice.

Ash moved ahead of them, nose down, body no longer loose with puppy enthusiasm but sharpened into something deliberate. He stopped often, scanning the bank before moving again, checking behind him as if ensuring they hadn't fallen away.

"He's mapping," Tom murmured.

"Yes," Alice replied. "And learning what not to trust."

The ground near the waterline felt unstable beneath her boots - not soft, but unreliable. The soil had been compacted once, pressed flat and told to behave normally again. Alice widened her stance instinctively, weight shifting as she tested it.

"You alright?" Tom asked.

"Yes," she said. "Just remembering."

The reeds near the bend leaned inward, bent without being broken. Alice noticed immediately - the way the stalks parted just enough to allow passage without leaving obvious damage.

"Someone's walked through here," she said.

Tom crouched, brushing his fingers lightly across the stems. "Not rushed."

"No," Alice agreed. "Not chased."

Ash sneezed sharply and backed away, ears flattening. He circled once, uncertain, then returned to Alice's side and pressed against her leg.

"That smell again," Tom said.

"Waterlogged," Alice replied. "And something else."

They stood in silence for a moment, the creek murmuring beside them like it had nothing to hide.

Alice didn't believe it.

They followed the bank downstream, the air thickening as trees crowded closer together. The smell intensified - eucalyptus layered over rot and time. Alice felt a familiar tightness between her shoulder blades, the sensation of stepping somewhere she'd once been redirected away from without explanation.

"I wasn't allowed here," she said suddenly.

Tom glanced at her. "Here?"

"This section," Alice replied. "It was never said outright. Just... managed."

"By who?"

She thought of her father's silences. Of adults who stopped talking when she entered a room. "Everyone."

Ash slowed again, body stiffening. He paused every few steps to look back, ensuring both of them were still behind him.

"He's keeping us together," Tom said quietly.

"Yes," Alice replied. "He's learned the rule already."

Ash broke away suddenly.

Not bolting - deciding.

He moved straight toward the bank, stopping short of the water, head tilted, eyes fixed on the mud near the edge. His body went rigid, tail frozen mid-line.

"Ash," Alice said softly.

He didn't respond.

Instead, he sat - hard and deliberate - staring at the ground as if daring it to explain itself.

Alice crouched beside him. "What've you found, mate?"

Ash nudged the mud once with his nose, then jumped back, startled by the contact.

The phone was wedged into the bank at a wrong angle.

Not dropped. Not lost. Forced.

Alice's stomach dropped as she picked it up carefully. Mud slid off in thick ribbons, the casing warped, the screen spiderwebbed with cracks radiating from a single point of impact.

"This isn't an accident," Tom said quietly.

Alice turned the phone over. The SIM tray hung open.

Empty.

"They removed it," she said. "Or he did - knowing it wouldn't matter."

Ash whined softly and sat again, gaze flicking toward the trees on the opposite bank.

Alice followed his line of sight.

Nothing moved.

But the air felt compressed - like it did before a storm or before something broke.

They didn't leave immediately.

That surprised Alice - the old instinct to retreat, to contain, to defer - but she stayed where she was, holding the phone like proof that refused to be explained away.

"This is the first thing they missed," she said.

Tom looked at her sharply. "Missed?"

"Yes." Her voice steadied as she spoke. "They erased records. They cleaned up sites. They managed people. But this—" She lifted the phone slightly. "This is careless."

"Or rushed," Tom said.

"Which means something changed," Alice replied.

Ash growled - low, steady, unafraid.

Tom's posture shifted instantly. "What is it?"

Ash stood and placed himself slightly in front of Alice, body angled toward the scrub. He didn't bark. He didn't retreat.

He held ground.

Alice felt a slow, cold awareness settle into her chest.

"He's telling us we've stayed long enough," she said.

Tom scanned the tree line. "Or that we're being timed."

They moved back toward the ute then - not running, not hurrying - but deliberately loud. Boots crunching. Branches snapping. A message without words.

Ash kept glancing over his shoulder, ears pricked.

Halfway back, Alice stopped.

Tom turned. "What?"

"This place," she said slowly. "It wasn't chosen because it's hidden."

Tom waited.

"It was chosen because it's ordinary," she continued. "People walk past it every day and don't look twice."

Tom's jaw tightened. "Until someone makes them."

Alice nodded. "Until now."

At the ute, Tom set the phone in the tray like it might explode if handled carelessly. He slammed the tailgate harder than necessary.

"This isn't just history," he said. "This is ongoing."

Alice leaned against the metal, letting the cold ground her. Her hands shook slightly now, the adrenaline finally catching up.

"They didn't expect anyone to come back and stay," she said.

Tom met her gaze. "They didn't expect *you*."

Ash jumped into the cab and curled up immediately, eyes still alert, body tense beneath the surface calm.

As Tom started the engine, Alice looked back toward the creek.

The reeds had settled again. The water ran on. Nothing about it looked dangerous. That was the problem.

Because the land had already given something back.

And it wouldn't stop there.

CHAPTER SEVEN

Alice woke to the wrong kind of quiet.

Not the honest quiet of night settling - the sort that carried crickets and wind and the distant shift of water - but a pressed silence, dense and deliberate, as if the world had been told to hold still.

For a moment she didn't know where she was.

Cold bit through her shoulder. The concrete floor stole warmth from her cheek. The smell was oil and dust, metallic at the back of her throat - the stale breath of a place that wasn't meant to hold people.

Then memory snapped into place with a sickening clarity.

The shed. The torch. The door closing without drama.

And the worst part - the part that made her chest tighten so hard she could barely breathe - was the thought that arrived immediately after.

Ash.

"Ash," she whispered, the sound too small in the dark.

A low whine answered her, close enough to feel.

Relief hit fast and fierce, dizzying in its intensity. Small claws scrabbled on concrete. A warm body pressed into her ribs, trembling. Ash shoved his head under her chin as if he could physically wedge fear away from her throat.

"It's alright," Alice murmured, one hand finding him, fingers sinking into soft fur. "Good boy. Good."

She forced herself to sit up slowly, keeping her movements measured. Panic made you loud. Panic made you clumsy. Whoever had done this hadn't rushed - which meant they weren't afraid of her reaction.

That was the detail that made her blood run colder.

Moonlight slipped through gaps in the corrugated iron, laying pale stripes across the floor. It wasn't enough to see clearly, but enough to confirm the shape of the door.

She crawled the last metre and reached for the handle.

It didn't move.

Alice tried again, harder this time. The latch held fast, unmoving. Not jammed. Secured.

Her breath fogged in the narrow beam of moonlight.

She pressed her forehead against the metal for a second, feeling the chill seep into her skin, then pulled back and forced herself to think.

Inventory. Options. Time.

She patted her pockets automatically, though she already knew.

No phone.

She remembered setting it on the ute tray. Remembered the small, casual act of leaving it behind. It hadn't felt important at the time.

Now it felt like a hand wrapped around her throat.

Tom had the phone, then. Tom would notice.

Unless—

No. Don't go there.

She turned away from the door and let her eyes adjust again, scanning the shed in strips of light. The workbench was a darker bulk against the far wall. Tools hung in careful order. Not the random mess of an old shed left to rust - but arranged. Maintained. Controlled.

Someone had been using this space. Recently.

Ash stayed close, moving with her, shoulder brushing her calf. He wasn't barking. He wasn't panicking. He was vibrating with contained alarm, like he was waiting for a cue.

Alice swallowed, tasting dust. "Alright," she whispered. "We're thinking, mate."

She moved slowly along the wall, one palm skimming the rough corrugation. The shed had a rhythm to it - gaps where air flowed, places where spiders had built and rebuilt webs over years. But under that, there were fresh disturbances. A scuff. A drag mark. The faint imprint of a boot sole in the dust where no one would have reason to walk unless they were doing something deliberate.

She crouched and touched the mark lightly, fingertips gritty.

Not old.

Her pulse kicked harder.

Ash's nose lifted, scenting the air. He let out a low, frustrated sound and moved toward the back corner - the same corner he'd marked earlier in the day - and sat down hard.

The exact same behaviour.

Alice stared at him.

"Ash..." she whispered.

He didn't look away. Didn't blink. He stared at the base of the wall like it had offended him.

Alice crawled toward him, the cold of the floor sinking into her knees. In the moonlight, she saw it - a narrow gap where the concrete met dirt, just wide enough for a small body to wriggle through. It wasn't an accident. The edge looked worn, used, as if something had passed through it more than once.

Her throat tightened.

Ash nudged the gap once, then looked up at her, tail still.

He wasn't asking permission.

He was offering her a way out of this that didn't include brute force.

"No," Alice whispered automatically. "You're not leaving me."

Ash whined, urgent now, and nudged the gap again. Then he pressed his head into her hand, hard, as if trying to push her decision into place.

Alice's chest hurt.

If Ash stayed, they were both trapped. If Ash went, he could find Tom.

But she'd only had him for days. He was a puppy. He could get lost. He could get hit on the road. He could—

She caught herself.

Tom had brought him here because he believed the pup would live. Because he believed the pup would be brave.

And Ash had already proved it.

Alice cupped his face in both hands, thumbs brushing his cheeks. His eyes were dark and steady, too serious for his age. He licked her wrist once, frantic and warm.

"You go," she whispered, voice breaking around the words. "You hear me? You go find him."

Ash's ears flattened. He whined again, like he hated the idea.

Alice pressed her forehead to his. "Please."

For a heartbeat, he stayed - torn, trembling.

Then he squeezed his body into the gap with a small grunt, claws scrabbling in the dirt. His tail vanished last, a whip of black disappearing into the night.

Alice sat back against the wall, alone.

The quiet closed in around her, thick and immediate without the puppy's warm body breaking it. She forced her breathing slow, counting in her head.

In. Hold. Out.

The shed didn't feel like a place now. It felt like an idea.

Containment.

Someone wanted her here because it proved they could put her here.

She listened.

Minutes stretched and warped. Time stopped behaving properly. Every sound grew teeth.

Once, a branch scraped against iron and she nearly bolted upright. Another time, something moved outside - a soft shift of gravel, too light to be a kangaroo, too careful to be wind.

Alice held her breath, body rigid, heart hammering against her ribs.

Footsteps passed close to the door.

Not fast. Not searching. Just... passing.

As if whoever it was knew exactly where she was and didn't need to check.

Her stomach rolled.

Then the steps moved away again, and silence returned.

She exhaled slowly, shaking.

This wasn't about hurting her. Not tonight.

This was about reminding her what the town could do when it wanted to.

About making her picture the next step.

Hours later - or minutes, it was impossible to tell - Ash barked in the distance.

Alice's whole body went tight.

Again.
Sharp. Repeated. Insistent.

Relief struck so hard she felt nauseous.

Then another sound joined it, heavier and faster - boots hitting gravel with urgency. A man running.

Tom.

"Alice!" His voice cut through the dark, raw with panic he hadn't tried to hide.

"Ash," she whispered, and then, louder, "Tom! I'm here!"

The lock didn't survive the second kick.

Metal screamed. The door crashed inward. Torchlight flooded the shed, harsh and blinding after darkness. Tom's silhouette filled the doorway like a force of nature, Ash skidding in behind him, barking like he was furious at the entire world.

Tom crossed the space in two strides and dropped in front of her, hands gripping her shoulders, searching her face with frantic precision.

"Are you hurt?" His voice broke on the word.

Alice shook her head quickly. "No. I'm okay."

He exhaled like something inside him gave way and pulled her hard against his chest. The hold was not gentle. It was protective in the most primal way - as if he could fuse her to him and make sure she stayed real.

Ash squeezed himself into the space between them, whining and licking Alice's hands, tail whipping against the concrete, frantic with relief.

Tom's hand slid up the back of her head, fingers tangled in her hair. "I shouldn't have left you."

"You shouldn't have had to," Alice said into his shoulder.

Tom pulled back just enough to look at her properly, eyes bright with anger and fear and something dangerously close to loss.

"They locked you in."

"Yes."

"How long?"

Alice swallowed. "Long enough."

Tom's jaw tightened. "This stops."

Alice met his gaze steadily. The adrenaline had burned down into something colder, heavier.

"Yes," she said. "It does."

Tom looked down at Ash, who stood pressed against Alice's leg, still trembling but proud, like he'd done exactly what he was born to do.

"You did good," Tom said hoarsely.

Ash licked his hand once and leaned back into Alice.

Alice knelt and wrapped an arm around the puppy, pressing her cheek briefly to his head. "You saved me," she whispered.

Ash's tail thumped once, firm and certain.

Outside, the night tried to settle back into place - pretending nothing had happened.

But Taravale had crossed a line.

And this time, Alice felt it in her bones.

Containment wasn't a warning anymore.

It was a message.

And she intended to answer it.

CHAPTER EIGHT

Alice didn't sleep.

She lay on top of the covers in the dark, fully dressed except for her boots, because the idea of being tangled in fabric felt too close to being trapped. The house was quiet - the kind of quiet it had always carried - but tonight it sounded different. Hollow in places it hadn't been before. Every creak of timber felt like a question.

Tom had locked the doors twice.

Not theatrically. Not angrily. Just methodically, as if locking things would return the world to its proper order. She'd watched him do it without speaking, her mind lagging behind her body, still half in the shed, still listening for footsteps that moved with certainty.

Ash lay on the rug beside the bed, chin on his paws, eyes wide open.

He wasn't sleeping either.

Every time a sound came from outside - wind through trees, a branch tapping iron - his ears lifted and his gaze snapped to the door. Then he looked back at Alice, like he was checking she was still there. Still breathing. Still in the room.

"You did good," she whispered, voice rough.

Ash's tail thumped once. Not happy. Not playful. Just acknowledgment.

Tom stood in the doorway for a moment, watching them.

"You should take your boots off," he said quietly.

Alice shook her head. "I don't want to."

Tom didn't argue. He stepped into the room and crouched beside Ash, rubbing the pup's neck with slow pressure. Ash leaned into it, then immediately repositioned himself closer to Alice again, as if Tom's touch was allowed only briefly.

Tom's mouth twitched. "He's decided."

Alice swallowed. "He's not wrong."

Tom's eyes lifted to hers, expression unreadable in the low light. "Do you want me in here?"

It wasn't the question she expected.

It wasn't *Can I stay?* or *Are you alright?* - because those were too small, too practical.

It was permission. It was respect. It was Tom asking her to choose the shape of the night.

Alice stared at him for a beat, then nodded once. "Yes."

Tom exhaled like he'd been holding something back. He didn't climb into the bed. He sat on the floor with his back against the wall, knees bent, forearms resting across them. Close enough that she could hear him breathe. Far enough that he wasn't crowding.

It was exactly what she needed.

Minutes passed. Maybe hours. Time didn't behave properly anymore.

Alice stared at the ceiling and tried to make her mind do something normal - count, plan, list. But it kept slipping back to the shed: the chill of the concrete, the taste of dust, the footsteps outside the door that didn't hurry.

Not searching.

Knowing.

Her stomach tightened again, and she realised her hands were clenched so hard her fingers hurt.

Tom's voice came quietly into the dark. "They came close."

Alice's throat worked. "Yes."

"How close?"

She hesitated. "Near enough that I could hear gravel shift. Near enough that they could've opened the door if they wanted."

Tom's breath hitched. The sound was small, but it made something in Alice's chest loosen - proof that he wasn't untouched by it. That he wasn't carrying this like a task.

"You didn't call out," Tom said.

"No." Her voice was thin. "I didn't want them to know what I sounded like."

Tom went very still.

After a moment he said, "They wanted you to feel helpless."

Alice turned her head slightly. In the moonlight, she could just make out the line of his profile. "They wanted me to imagine what happens next time."

Tom's jaw tightened. "There won't be a next time."

Alice almost laughed - not because it was funny, but because it was the kind of promise people made right before the world proved them arrogant. Still, she wanted it. Wanted something to hold.

"I don't want you making promises you can't keep," she said.

Tom's voice was flat, controlled. "Then let me make a promise I can."

Alice swallowed. "Alright."

"I will not leave you alone again," Tom said. "Not while this is active."

The words settled in the room like a weight. Not romantic. Not dramatic. Practical and fierce.

Alice closed her eyes. "Okay."

Ash stood and climbed up onto the bed, circling twice before settling hard against her hip, his warm body anchoring her in place. He pressed his nose into her ribs with a soft huff, then sighed like he was finally allowing himself to rest.

Alice rested her hand on his back, fingers splayed wide.

"His name suits him," she whispered.

Tom's breath softened. "Ash?"

"Yes." Her voice thickened. "Because everything feels... burnt."

Tom didn't respond immediately.

Then, quietly: "Burnt things still grow back."

Alice's eyes stung. She blinked hard, refusing to let tears turn this into something she couldn't control.

"Does it ever stop feeling like this?" she asked.

Tom's answer came without hesitation. "Yes."

She waited.

"It stops feeling like panic," he clarified. "It becomes vigilance. You learn the difference."

Alice's throat tightened. "I don't want to live like a hunted thing."

Tom's voice darkened. "You're not hunted."

Alice looked toward him in the dark. "Then what am I?"

Tom shifted slightly, the boards whispering under his weight. "You're inconvenient."

The word made her huff a breath - not a laugh, but close.

Tom continued, steadier now. "You're the kind of person who makes lies expensive."

Alice stared at the ceiling again, letting the sentence sink into her bones.

Outside, the wind picked up slightly, rattling a loose piece of guttering. Ash's ears flicked, but he didn't lift his head. Tom didn't move. The sound passed.

For a moment, the world felt almost normal.

Alice's body, however, refused to forget.

She could still feel the cold in her shoulder. The ache in her knees. The wrongness of being contained.

Tom must have heard her breathing change, because his voice came again, lower. "Tell me what you need."

The question struck her harder than the shed had.

Because it wasn't *What happened?* or *Are you okay?* - it was an offering. A hand held out without trying to pull her anywhere.

Alice swallowed. "I need... to not be touched like I'm fragile."

Tom's answer was immediate. "Okay."

"And I need," she continued, voice steadier, "to not be brave for everyone."

Tom's eyes lifted to hers, dark in the moonlight. "You don't have to be."

Alice stared at him for a beat, then nodded once.

Ash shifted, pressed closer, a warm weight that insisted she stayed here, present.

Tom stayed on the floor.

Not leaving. Not pushing. Just holding the line.

In the early hours - when the sky began to pale and the land slowly exhaled into morning - Alice finally drifted into something like sleep, the edges of her mind still sharp, but her body easing under the certainty of two beings beside her who refused to let the night swallow her whole.

Outside, Taravale was quiet again.

Not innocent.

Waiting.

And inside the old stone house at Taravale, Alice wasn't safe yet - but she was no longer alone in the dark.

CHAPTER NINE

Morning came cautiously.

Light slid across the paddocks in thin bands, pale and uncertain, as if the land itself wasn't convinced it was safe to fully arrive yet. Alice stood on the verandah with a mug cooling in her hands, watching frost lift slowly from the grass. Her body ached in the quiet way it did after adrenaline had burned too hot, too fast.

Ash sat pressed against her shin, warm and solid, head up, eyes tracking the road with unwavering focus. He hadn't slept properly since the shed. Neither had she.

Behind her, Tom moved through the house with deliberate care - checking doors, checking windows, checking the world back into something that made sense. The sound of him grounding the space steadied her more than the tea ever could.

"They wanted me to imagine the next step," Alice said quietly.

Tom paused at the doorway. "They wanted you measuring it."

She nodded. "How easy it would be. How quiet."

Tom leaned against the post beside her, jaw darkened with stubble he hadn't bothered shaving. "And did it work?"

Alice thought of the footsteps outside the shed. The casualness of them. The certainty.

"No," she said. "It clarified things."

Ash's tail thumped once in agreement.

Tom crouched and rested a hand briefly on the pup's back. "You're not leaving her side today."

Ash glanced up at him like that instruction was unnecessary.

They went into town late morning.

Not to ask questions. Not to explain. To be seen.

Ash rode in the cab, chin braced against the window, watching the road with a seriousness that felt far beyond his weeks. Alice noticed people noticed him first - then Tom - then her.

Conversations faltered.

At the shop, Linda's smile arrived a second too late.

"You look tired," she said.

Alice met her gaze evenly. "I was locked in a shed overnight."

The words landed hard between them.

Linda's mouth opened. Closed. "That's... not funny."

"I didn't say it was."

Linda swallowed. "People are saying you shouldn't be out on your own."

Tom stepped closer to the counter, presence unmistakable. "She wasn't."

Linda's eyes flicked between them, then down to Ash. "You've got a lot going on."

"That's true," Alice said. "But it doesn't make me wrong."

Linda rang up their items too quickly, hands shaking just enough to notice.

Outside, the street felt tighter than it had the day before - not hostile exactly, but alert. Watchful in the way people became when they were waiting to see who would blink first.

At the post office, the woman behind the counter didn't speak at all. She slid the mail across and turned away, shoulders stiff.

"That's new," Tom murmured as they stepped back into the sunlight.

"She's been told not to engage," Alice replied. "Engagement creates memory."

Ash barked once at a man loitering near the servo, the sound sharp and unapologetic. The man stepped back instinctively.

Tom hid a smile.

They drove the long way home, dust rising behind them like a marker drawn deliberately. Alice rested her hand on Ash's back, grounding herself in the steady heat of him.

"I don't think they expected you to come back," she said.

Tom kept his eyes on the road. "They hoped I wouldn't."

"That changes things."

"Yes."

Back at the house, Tom fixed the shed door properly - not loudly, not angrily. Just enough that it wouldn't close the same way again. Alice watched from the doorway, Ash at her feet.

"They measured me," she said. "Last night."

Tom straightened, resting his forearms on the fence rail. "And now?"

"And now I'm measuring them back."

Tom turned to face her fully. "This gets harder from here."

"I know."

"They won't stop trying to make you doubt yourself."

Alice met his gaze without flinching. "I don't need certainty anymore. I need momentum."

Something shifted in Tom then - a final piece clicking into place. He stepped closer, cupped her face with both hands, forehead resting against hers.

"You're not doing this alone," he said quietly. "Not now. Not again."

Alice closed her eyes, breathing him in - dust, sun, familiarity. "I don't want careful," she said. "I want honest."

Tom kissed her then - slow, grounding, deliberate. Not urgency. Commitment.

Ash sat heavily at their feet, offended at being excluded, then leaned against Alice's leg with a small huff.

When they broke apart, Alice rested her forehead briefly against Tom's chest, listening to his heart steady and strong beneath her ear.

"They crossed a line," she said.

Tom's hand slid to the back of her neck, thumb pressing lightly there. "So did we."

Ash stood and trotted toward the fence, ears pricked, attention caught by something beyond the rise. He didn't bark - just watched.

Alice followed his gaze. The land lay open, brittle and bright, pretending nothing had changed.

But she knew better now. Because silence had failed. And Taravale was about to learn what came after.

CHAPTER TEN

The first thing to disappear was the record.

Alice noticed it because she wasn't looking for it.

She was at the dining table with Daniel Bennett's name written at the top of a page, mapping dates she already knew by heart. Fuel. Parcel. Phone. The shape of his last forty-eight hours had become familiar, a pattern she could trace even when she closed her eyes.

When she checked the council website again, the entry she'd screenshot the night before was gone.

Not altered.

Gone.

She refreshed the page twice. Then once more, slower, like that might make a difference.

Nothing.

"Tom," she said.

He looked up from the sink where he was rinsing a mug. Ash lay stretched out between them, chin on his paws, eyes flicking up at the change in her voice.

"What?"

"The access permit," Alice said. "The temporary one issued three weeks ago. It was there last night."

Tom crossed the room and leaned over her shoulder. "And now?"

"And now it never existed."

Tom straightened slowly. "That's fast."

"That's practiced."

Ash stood and moved closer, positioning himself against Alice's knee without looking at her, gaze fixed on the doorway like he was tracking something that hadn't made a sound.

She clicked through other pages.

Fuel records - incomplete. The post office register - scanned, not original. Council minutes - amended without notation.

They weren't destroying evidence.

They were **editing reality**.

Alice closed the laptop carefully. "This isn't panic."

Tom nodded. "No. This is clean-up."

She rubbed her temples. "They've done this before."

Tom didn't argue. He didn't need to.

They went back into town after lunch.

Again, not to confront.

To confirm.

At the post office, the woman behind the counter didn't smile at all this time.

"I need to see the registered parcel log from three weeks ago," Alice said.

The woman's hands froze. "Why?"

"Because I saw it yesterday."

"No, you didn't."

The certainty in her voice was worse than denial.

"I did," Alice said evenly. "Daniel Bennett signed for it."

The woman's eyes flicked briefly to Tom - then away. "There was no Daniel Bennett."

The words sat between them, deliberate and final.

Tom leaned on the counter. "You're saying she imagined a signature?"

"I'm saying," the woman replied, voice clipped, "that sometimes people mistake what they want to see for what's actually there."

Ash growled.

Not loud.

Not threatening.

Just enough to be heard.

The woman's gaze dropped to the dog, then lifted again, harder now. "You shouldn't bring animals in here."

Alice slid her hand down Ash's back, steadying him. "You shouldn't lie."

The woman straightened. "You're not welcome to go through records without cause."

Alice nodded. "Then I'll find cause."

Outside, the street felt hostile in a quieter way than before. Less watching. More avoidance.

At the servo, the pumps were busy, but no one met her eyes. At the shop, Linda rang her up quickly and handed over the receipt without a word.

The town wasn't pushing back anymore.

It was closing ranks.

They drove home in silence, dust trailing behind them like a line drawn carefully back to the house.

Inside, Tom shut the door and locked it.

"This is what they do," Alice said. "They don't argue facts. They erase them."

Tom leaned against the bench, arms crossed. "They're betting you won't trust your own memory."

"They're wrong," she said.

Tom followed her gaze. "About more than one thing."

Alice picked up her notebook and turned to a clean page. Wrote the date. The time. What had changed. What hadn't.

"They can alter systems," she said. "But they can't alter the land."

Tom's mouth curved grimly. "That's where they always get caught."

Ash stood suddenly, hackles lifting just enough to notice.

A vehicle passed on the road. Didn't slow. Didn't stop.

But it circled the block.

Alice closed the notebook.

"This has happened before," she said quietly. "Daniel wasn't the first."

Tom met her eyes. "Then he won't be the last - unless we stop it."

Alice nodded once.

Outside, Taravale settled into its afternoon stillness, neat and untroubled on the surface.

Inside the old stone house, the truth took shape.

And this time, it wasn't going to be written out.

CHAPTER ELEVEN

The photographs had been tucked away carefully.

That was the first thing Alice noticed when she spread them across the dining table again - not the images themselves, but the way they'd been handled. Flattened. Protected. Not the treatment of something shameful or impulsive, but of something important.

Tom stood opposite her, arms folded, eyes fixed on the face that stared back from the centre print.

"He knew him," Tom said.

Alice nodded. "Not well. But enough."

The man in the photos hadn't changed since Alice last looked. Same steady gaze. Same half-turn of the shoulders, caught mid-movement like he'd been interrupted.

"What I missed before," she said slowly, "is the timing."

She slid Daniel Bennett's notes out beside the photographs. Dates. Locations. Questions written in a tight, impatient hand.

"He came back here after this," Alice continued. "After the man in the photos died."

Tom's jaw tightened. "Which means he wasn't chasing a rumour."

"No," Alice said. "He was chasing an answer."

Ash lay under the table, head resting on his paws, eyes open now. He hadn't settled properly since town. Every so often, his ears twitched toward the road, as if he was listening to something too distant for them to hear.

Alice turned one photograph sideways. "Look at this."

Tom leaned in. "What am I looking for?"

"The background," she said. "That fence line doesn't exist anymore."

Tom frowned. "You're sure?"

"I am," Alice replied. "It was replaced after the fire. The one everyone says didn't matter."

Tom straightened. "That was twenty years ago."

"Yes," Alice said. "And it's when the man in the photos stopped talking."

Silence settled between them.

Ash stood suddenly and moved closer, placing his front paws lightly against Alice's knee. She rested a hand on his head without looking down.

"They said Daniel drifted," Alice said. "They said the man in the photos drank. They said both of them were unreliable."

Tom's voice was quiet. "And now one of them is dead."

Alice met his gaze. "And one of them is missing."

Tom exhaled slowly. "Or hasn't been found yet."

The word landed hard.

Alice pushed the photographs together, stacking them carefully again. "Daniel came back because he realised this wasn't a single story."

"He thought if he could prove a pattern—"

"He could break it," Alice finished.

Ash let out a low sound in his chest, almost a warning.

Outside, a ute passed. Too slow. Too deliberate.

Tom moved to the window and watched it disappear down the road. "We don't leave him like this."

"No," Alice agreed. "We don't."

She gathered the papers and slid them into a folder, then reached for her notebook and wrote a single line at the top of a clean page.

NOT THE FIRST.

Below it, she added another.

NOT THE LAST - UNLESS.

Tom watched her write. "You're thinking about the old fire."

"I'm thinking about what it covered," she said. "And what people got very good at explaining away afterward."

Ash pressed closer, his small body solid and warm against her leg.

Tom rested his hand briefly on Alice's shoulder. "We find where Daniel went next."

Alice nodded. "And we don't announce it."

She closed the folder and slid it out of sight.

Outside, the land lay open and quiet, pretending not to remember.

But Alice knew better now.

Because some men didn't disappear.

They followed a trail someone else had already walked - and never come back from.

CHAPTER TWELVE

The pump shed sat lower than Alice remembered.

Or maybe she had remembered it as smaller - less significant - the way children did with structures that weren't meant for them. Now, standing above it again, she could see how deliberately it had been placed: tucked just out of sight from the house, shielded by a bend in the land that funneled sound away from the road.

Private.
Useful.
Forgettable.

Ash didn't like it.

He slowed as they approached, tail lowering, nose lifting as if scenting something that didn't belong to the present. He circled wide, then stopped abruptly and sat, ears forward, gaze fixed on the corrugated iron door.

"That's new," Tom said quietly.

Alice nodded. "He's learned what no longer pretends."

The shed door hung crooked on its hinges, rust bleeding down the metal like old injuries. The lock had been cut cleanly - not snapped, not forced. Removed.

Tom stepped in front of Alice instinctively. "Stay back."

She didn't argue, but she didn't retreat either.

The smell hit them first.

Not rot - not yet - but damp iron, old oil, stagnant water. A place that had been sealed and then reopened without care for what might remain.

Ash let out a low whine and pressed against Alice's leg, body tense but steady.

Tom pushed the door open.

It screamed.

The sound ripped across the paddocks, raw and exposed, far louder than the shed deserved. Alice flinched despite herself, heart jumping into her throat. The sound lingered too long, echoing off land that had heard worse and remembered it.

Inside, the light was wrong.

It slanted through gaps in the iron, cutting the space into sharp, uneven shapes. Dust motes hung suspended in the air like they were afraid to settle.

The pump itself stood silent in the centre, pipes running down into the ground like veins. A hose lay coiled nearby, carefully - deliberately - not discarded.

Alice stepped inside despite Tom's hand lifting slightly, hesitation flickering across his face before he let it fall.

She stopped three steps in.

"This isn't maintenance," she said.

Tom followed her gaze.

The floor had been cleaned.

Not thoroughly. Not professionally. But enough - enough to remove obvious evidence, enough to convince someone who didn't want to look too closely.

Ash growled.

This time it was louder.

"Easy, mate," Tom murmured, but Ash didn't ease. He moved forward, placing himself between Alice and the far wall.

That was when she saw it.

The disturbed soil near the base of the pump - darker, heavier, damp in a way the rest of the floor wasn't. It hadn't been dug recently. It had been opened, then closed again.

"They didn't want to leave him here," Alice said quietly.

Tom's jaw tightened. "But they did."

Alice crouched slowly, fingers brushing the ground. The earth was compacted - pressed flat by weight, then abandoned.

"This was temporary," she said. "A holding place."

Tom swallowed. "Jesus."

Ash whined again, pacing now, nails clicking against concrete as his agitation grew.

Alice stood abruptly. "He was alive when he came here."

Tom looked at her sharply. "What makes you say that?"

"Because this isn't panic," she replied. "This is organisation. You don't organise around something that's already done."

The silence inside the shed thickened.

Alice felt it then - the shape of what had happened - not as a narrative, but as a series of decisions made by people who thought they were entitled to make them.

She turned slowly, scanning the walls.

There.

A scrape, faint but deliberate, just above the floor - something dragged sideways, not down. A body moved, not dropped.

Her breath caught.

Tom followed her gaze. "Alice..."

"They thought the water would erase it," she said. "Movement. Noise. Utility."

Ash barked sharply, sudden and final.

The sound echoed violently off the iron walls.

Tom swore under his breath. "We shouldn't be here alone."

Alice nodded. "We're not."

The realisation landed cold and heavy.

Someone had stood here before them - not long ago - checking, adjusting, making sure the shed still behaved.

Tom reached for Alice's arm. "We go."

They didn't argue this time.

As they backed out into the daylight, Alice glanced once more at the pump shed.

It looked ordinary again.

That was its purpose.

And it had served it well.

CHAPTER THIRTEEN

They didn't speak on the drive back.

Not because there was nothing to say - but because everything that mattered had already been decided.

Ash lay on the seat between them, chin resting on Alice's thigh, eyes half-closed but alert. Every now and then his ears flicked, tracking sounds beyond the cab, checking the world was still where it belonged.

The house felt wrong when they arrived. Too open. Too exposed.

Tom locked the door behind them without comment.

Alice went straight to the sink and washed her hands until the water ran cold, then colder. Dirt spiralled down the drain, stubborn as memory. When she finally stopped, she rested her palms flat on the bench and breathed.

"He's dead," she said.

Tom didn't argue it. He stood a few steps back, arms crossed, watching her carefully. "Yes."

"And they're going to pretend he never existed."

"Yes."

She turned then, eyes bright but steady. "I won't let them."

Tom nodded once. "I figured."

Ash whined softly and stood, moving closer to Alice, pressing his shoulder into her leg. She rested a hand on his back, grounding herself in the warmth of him.

"They didn't just kill him," Alice continued. "They erased him. Same as the man in the photos. Same as whoever came before that."

Tom exhaled slowly. "It's a system."

"And systems don't stop on their own."

"No."

She crossed the room and pulled the folder from the drawer, laying it out on the table with care. Photographs. Notes. Dates. Daniel's handwriting sharp and insistent beside her own.

"They've been doing this for years," she said. "Long enough to get good at it."

Tom leaned over her shoulder. "And sloppy enough to leave traces."

Alice met his gaze. "Which means we move fast."

"Carefully."

"Publicly," she said.

Tom's jaw tightened. "That will provoke them."

"Yes," Alice agreed. "That's the point."

Silence stretched between them, heavy but not uncertain.

Tom reached out and cupped her face, thumb brushing beneath her eye. "If we do this, there's no stepping back."

"I know."

"And they won't stop trying to scare you."

Alice leaned into his touch. "They already crossed that line."

Tom rested his forehead against hers for a moment, breathing her in like he needed the reminder she was here, alive, unbroken.

"Alright," he said quietly. "Then we change the rules."

Ash barked once, sharp and decisive, as if approving the plan.

Alice huffed a breath that was almost a laugh. "You're on the wrong side of history, mate."

Ash wagged his tail once, unapologetic.

They spent the afternoon working - not frantically, not emotionally. Methodically. Alice wrote everything down by hand, twice. Dates. Times. Places. What could be erased digitally was anchored on paper instead.

As dusk crept in, Tom stepped outside to check the perimeter. Alice stayed at the table, Ash sprawled at her feet, notebook open in front of her.

She stopped writing when a name surfaced again.

Not Daniel's.

The other one.

The man in the photographs.

She circled it slowly, deliberately.

"This is where it connects," she murmured.

Ash lifted his head.

A sound drifted in from outside - a vehicle slowing on the road, then moving on.

Tom came back inside, closing the door carefully. "We're not invisible anymore."

Alice nodded. "Good."

She closed the notebook and rested her hand flat over it.

"They think I'll get tired," she said. "Or frightened enough to stop."

Tom stepped closer, his presence solid, unyielding. "They don't know you."

Alice met his gaze, the truth of that settling calm and fierce in her chest.

"No," she said. "They really don't."

Outside, the land darkened into evening, patient as ever.

Inside the house at Taravale, the truth stopped being something that could be managed.

It became something that demanded an ending.

CHAPTER FOURTEEN

The rumour reached Alice before breakfast.

Not directly. Not cleanly. It arrived sideways, carried on politeness and lowered voices, wrapped in concern so careful it almost passed for kindness.

She heard it in Linda's tone at the shop - too gentle, too deliberate.

"People are worried about you," Linda said, not meeting her eyes as she slid a loaf of bread across the counter.

Alice paused. "Worried how?"

Linda hesitated, then sighed. "You've been through a lot. Anyone would struggle."

"That's not an answer."

Linda's mouth tightened. "They're saying you're seeing patterns that aren't there."

Alice smiled faintly. "Who's *they*?"

Linda glanced toward the back room. Toward the office. Toward somewhere Alice wasn't invited. "People who care."

Alice paid and walked out without another word.

Ash stayed close as they crossed the street, shoulder brushing her leg, his body a small, steady weight that reminded her she wasn't imagining the tension coiled through the town. He watched everyone. He missed nothing.

At the post office, the woman didn't speak to her at all. Simply handed over the mail and turned away.

The message was clear.

You're no longer neutral.

By lunchtime, Alice had heard three versions of the same story.

She   was   grieving.
She   was   fixated.
She had always been dramatic.

None of them were outright accusations. That would have required courage. Instead, they were suggestions - small, corrosive things designed to slip in quietly and lodge.

Tom listened without interrupting as Alice recounted it back at the house, his expression darkening with each repetition.

"They're setting you up," he said.

"Yes," Alice agreed. "They're making it social."

Ash growled softly from the doorway, ears pinned as a car slowed on the road outside.

Tom watched it pass. "They want you isolated."

"They want me doubting myself."

Tom met her gaze. "Are you?"

Alice thought of the shed door closing. The phone in the mud. The smell in the pump shed that wouldn't leave her memory.

"No," she said. "But they're hoping everyone else will."

Tom nodded. "Then we don't let them frame the story."

Alice leaned back against the bench. "We don't confront them either."

Tom frowned. "No?"

"They're waiting for that," she said. "They want reaction. Emotion. Something they can point to and say *See?*"

He considered that, then nodded slowly. "So what do we do?"

Alice reached for her notebook and flipped it open. "We let them talk."

Tom raised an eyebrow. "That sounds risky."

"It is," she said. "But people get careless when they think they've won."

Ash barked once, sharp and insistent, as if punctuating the thought.

Later that afternoon, Claire rang.

"I think someone went through Daniel's car," she said without preamble. "Nothing taken. Just… moved."

Alice closed her eyes. "They're checking what you know."

Claire's voice shook. "What do I do?"

"You stay where you are," Alice said firmly. "And you don't answer questions you weren't asked directly."

A pause. Then: "I'm scared."

"I know," Alice said softly. "So am I."

After the call ended, the house felt tighter. Smaller.

Tom reached for Alice's hand and squeezed once, steady and grounding. "They're pushing."

"Yes," Alice said. "Because we're close."

Ash trotted over and sat at their feet, gaze fixed on the door, body angled protectively toward Alice.

As dusk fell, Alice stood on the verandah and watched the light drain from the paddocks. Somewhere, a gate creaked. A dog barked and fell silent again.

Taravale wasn't shouting her down.

It was **rewriting her**.

Alice rested a hand on Ash's head, feeling the warmth of him, the solidity.

"They think if they make me small enough," she said quietly, "the truth will shrink with me."

Tom stepped up beside her. "They're wrong."

Alice nodded, eyes fixed on the darkening land.

"They always are."

CHAPTER FIFTEEN

The call came just after dark.

Alice almost didn't answer.

Not because she didn't recognise the number - she did - but because instinct told her it wasn't meant to help. It was meant to *move her*. Pull her out of the calm she'd been building and back into the town's undertow.

The phone buzzed again, insistent, like it knew she was watching it.

Ash lifted his head from the rug, ears pricked. He crossed the room and sat at Alice's feet, looking up at her face with steady attention. Not anxious. Not needy.

Ready.

Alice answered.

"Don't come looking tonight."

The voice was tight, breathless. Female. Familiar, but strained enough that it took Alice a beat to place it.

"Maggie," she said.

Silence on the line - the kind that wasn't empty, but loaded.

Then a shaky exhale. "You shouldn't have gone out there."

Alice stood slowly, moving away from the window as if distance might make the conversation safer. "Out where?"

"You know where."

"I do," Alice said evenly. "That's why I went."

Maggie made a sound that might've been a laugh if it hadn't cracked halfway through. "You don't understand what you're stepping into."

Alice's gaze flicked to Tom on the other side of the room. He'd gone still, posture shifting the moment he heard the name. He didn't interrupt. He didn't need to. His whole body was listening.

"Maggie," Alice said gently, "who's been speaking to you?"

A pause. Too long.

Maggie swallowed audibly. "People are asking questions."

"They already were," Alice replied.

"Yes, but—" Maggie broke off, voice dropping. "Not like this."

Ash's ears tipped forward. His body leaned toward the sound of the phone like he wanted to climb into it and make it stop.

Alice tightened her grip. "Who, Maggie?"

Maggie's breath hitched. "I can't say their names."

"You can," Alice said, calm and firm. "You're choosing not to."

That landed.

Maggie's voice turned small. "You don't get it. Here… if you say a name, it becomes your problem. It becomes your fault."

Alice closed her eyes for a second. "It's already your problem. They've made sure of that."

Maggie went quiet again - and in that quiet, Alice heard something else underneath it.

History.

Not just fear of *now*, but fear that had been practiced for years until it felt like the only sensible way to survive.

"Did you see Daniel?" Alice asked softly.

Silence.

Not denial. Not confusion.

Recognition.

"Maggie," Alice said, voice steady, "did you see him or not?"

"Yes."

The word fell heavy, final.

Tom's jaw tightened.

Alice kept her tone gentle. "When?"

"The night he came back," Maggie whispered. "He was at the hall. Late. After everyone else had left."

"What was he doing?" Tom asked quietly from across the room.

Alice held up a hand to him - not to stop him, but to keep the line clean.

Maggie spoke as if she could see the place again. "He was asking questions. Not loud. Not dramatic. Just... specific. About the old fire."

Alice's stomach tightened. "Which fire?"

Maggie's breath shook. "Not the one everyone talks about. The clean-up afterward. The paperwork no one keeps where it should be. Who signed what. Who decided what stayed buried and what got carted away."

Alice felt the pieces shift into place. The man in the photographs. The fence line that didn't exist anymore. The way records were disappearing now, quick and neat.

"Did anyone else see him?" Alice asked.

Maggie hesitated. "Yes."

Alice's voice sharpened slightly. "Who?"

"I can't," Maggie said quickly, panic rising. "If I say it—"

"They're already leaning on you," Alice said. "So tell me this instead: are they pretending they didn't see him?"

"Yes," Maggie whispered. "They're saying now he wasn't there."

Alice's expression didn't change. "And do you believe them?"

Maggie's breath caught. "No."

Outside, a car slowed on the road, engine idling a fraction too long before moving on.

Ash growled softly, deep in his chest.

Maggie heard something in the silence on the line and went quieter. "They've been around my place."

Alice's pulse quickened. "How?"

"Not knocking," Maggie said. "Just... there. A ute parked near the gate. A car turning at the end of the drive. Like they want me to notice without saying a word."

Alice pictured it instantly - the same tactic, the same measurement.

"They're checking if you'll fold," Alice said.

Maggie's voice broke. "I have kids, Alice."

The words were raw and simple, a truth that explained everything. Not weakness. Responsibility.

Alice softened. "I know."

Maggie swallowed hard. "Daniel said if anything happened to him, it wouldn't be an accident."

Alice's throat tightened. "Did he say why?"

"He said he'd found proof," Maggie whispered. "Not just about the man in the photos. About... a pattern. About things that kept happening to the wrong people."

A cold certainty settled behind Alice's ribs.

"And you didn't tell anyone," Alice said, not accusing - naming.

"I tried," Maggie whispered. "I tried to talk to someone and they looked at me like I'd sworn in church. Like I'd dragged something filthy into the light."

Tom's voice was low and controlled now. "Who told you to stop talking?"

Maggie went silent again. Then, very quietly: "Everyone."

The line hummed with it. The way a whole town could become a hand over your mouth without anyone ever touching you.

Alice's grip tightened on the phone. "Maggie, listen to me. You don't answer any more questions. Not from them. Not from anyone who 'just wants to check you're okay'. If someone comes to your place, you don't let them in."

Maggie's breath came fast. "I don't want trouble."

Alice's voice hardened, not unkindly. "Then stop helping them pretend this is normal."

A beat.

Maggie whispered, "What if they make me look crazy?"

Alice exhaled slowly. "They will try. That's what they do. But I'll hold the line. You won't be alone in it."

Maggie's breath hitched. "You can't promise that."

Alice stared at the dark window, seeing nothing and everything. "I'm promising you I won't disappear you."

The silence that followed was different. Not fear.

Relief - small, fragile, real.

Maggie whispered, "I can tell you one thing."

Alice's pulse steadied. "Yes."

"They're not just worried," Maggie said. "They're angry."

Alice closed her eyes. "Because we're close."

"Yes." Maggie's voice shook again. "And because Daniel didn't come back for nostalgia. He came back because he knew where to look."

The line went dead.

Alice stood very still, phone pressed to her ear, listening to nothing.

Tom was beside her before she realised he'd moved, his hand resting lightly on her arm, grounding. "You got what we needed."

Alice lowered the phone. "She's terrified."

Tom's jaw flexed. "Which means they're leaning on her hard."

"Yes," Alice said. "And she cracked."

Ash barked once, sharp and decisive, then settled at Alice's feet again, body angled toward the door.

Alice walked to the table and wrote Maggie's name down - not as a witness to be used, but as a person to be protected. Then she wrote:

HALL - LATE - QUESTIONS ABOUT CLEAN-UP

She circled it twice.

"They're not erasing anymore," Alice said quietly. "They're managing panic."

Tom looked at her. "Which makes them sloppy."

"Yes," Alice agreed. "And sloppy people make mistakes."

She closed the notebook and slid it away.

Outside, Taravale lay quiet, its neat explanations starting to buckle under their own weight.

And somewhere in that quiet, someone realised they'd lost control of the story.

Which made them dangerous.

CHAPTER SIXTEEN

Ash woke her.

Not with a bark - with weight.

He climbed onto the bed without invitation, paws landing squarely on Alice's chest, breath hot and urgent against her chin. His body trembled, every muscle tight.

"Ash?" she whispered.

He didn't move. His eyes were fixed on the doorway, ears flattened, listening.

Alice's heart kicked hard.

Beside her, Tom was already awake.

He slid out of bed without a sound, reaching for the torch on the bedside table. Ash growled low in his throat now, the sound vibrating through Alice's ribs.

Tom paused at the door.

Outside, gravel shifted.

Not footsteps. Tyres.

Tom met Alice's eyes in the half-light. Don't move.

Ash ignored that instruction entirely.

The puppy launched himself off the bed and bolted down the hallway, barking - loud, sharp, relentless. The sound shattered the quiet, echoing off stone and timber.

Tom swore and moved fast.

By the time Alice reached the front door, Ash was already there, hackles raised, teeth bared, a wall of noise and fury in a body that should not have been capable of it.

Headlights flared through the front windows.

A ute idled at the gate.

Then - panic.

The engine revved. Gravel sprayed. The headlights swung wildly, then vanished down the road.

Tom flung the door open and ran to the fence line, torch cutting through dust. Nothing left but churned earth and the smell of hot rubber.

Ash tore after him, barking into the dark, furious now, offended, alive.

Alice stood on the verandah, heart hammering, the cold biting through her skin. They waited a long moment before Tom came back.

"That wasn't a warning," he said grimly. "That was a test."

Ash pressed against Alice's legs, still shaking, tail low but determined.

"They wanted to see if we'd sleep," Alice said.

Tom nodded. "And if we'd be quiet."

Alice looked down at Ash, crouching to wrap her arms around his small, shaking body. "They won't try that again."

Tom crouched beside her, hand resting between Ash's shoulders, grounding all three of them. "No. Next time, they'll change tactics."

Inside, they locked the doors again - not out of fear, but awareness.

Sleep didn't return easily.

When morning came, Alice felt hollowed out and sharp all at once. The kind of clarity that followed adrenaline, when denial burned away.

"They're escalating," she said over breakfast.

Tom nodded. "Because they're running out of room."

Ash lay under the table, chin on his paws, eyes never fully closing.

Alice stared out the window toward the road. "They don't want exposure anymore."

"They want silence," Tom said. "Permanent."

Alice turned back to him, resolve settling hard and immovable.

"Then we end this," she said. "Before they decide someone else doesn't get to be remembered."

Ash lifted his head and barked once, fierce and certain.

And for the first time since Daniel Bennett disappeared, Alice knew this wasn't about uncovering the past anymore.

It was about surviving the present.

CHAPTER SEVENTEEN

The night pressed in early.

Cloud cover rolled across the valley and settled low, muting the moon and flattening sound. Alice noticed it the moment the light changed - the way the paddocks lost depth, the way the house felt closer to itself, walls drawing in as if they'd learned something new and weren't ready to share it yet.

Tom had been quiet since dinner.

Not withdrawn. Focused.

He moved through the kitchen with economy - rinsing a plate that didn't need rinsing, wiping the bench twice, checking the back door even though it was already bolted. Alice watched him from the table, the rhythm of his movements almost soothing, almost hypnotic.

Ash lay beneath her chair, chin on his paws, eyes tracking Tom with the seriousness of a dog who'd decided this man mattered.

"Sit down," Alice said finally.

Tom paused, hands braced on the sink. "In a minute."

Alice waited. The minute stretched.

She pushed her chair back and stood. "Tom."

He turned then, the carefulness she'd come to recognise still in place - but thinner now, worn at the edges.

"Alright," he said quietly, and crossed the room to sit opposite her. He didn't lean back. He didn't relax. He sat like this was a meeting with consequences.

Alice folded her hands on the table. "You don't think we should go."

Tom didn't argue it. "I think it's a bad room."

"That's not the same thing."

"No," he agreed. "It's worse."

Ash lifted his head, ears pricked, sensing the shift.

Alice took a breath. "Say it."

Tom rubbed a hand over his jaw, then let it fall. "I think they want us contained. Not physically this time. Socially. Narratively."

Alice nodded. "They already tried the first."

"Yes," Tom said. "Which means they'll escalate."

She met his gaze. "You're afraid."

The word hung between them.

Tom didn't flinch. "Yes."

Not fear *of* her decision - fear *for* her.

Alice exhaled slowly. "That's new."

"I've always been afraid," he said. "I just didn't let it speak."

Ash stood and moved closer to Alice's leg, pressing his shoulder against her shin, a quiet, grounding insistence.

Tom noticed. "He does that when you tense."

Alice glanced down, surprised. "I didn't realise I was."

Tom's mouth curved faintly. "You hide it better than you think."

The room went quiet again, the kind of quiet that wasn't empty but waiting.

Alice stood and walked to the window, looking out across the paddocks. The dark made the land feel limitless - dangerous in its openness.

"I almost didn't come back," she said.

Tom's head lifted. "I know."

"I told myself I'd finish what needed finishing and leave," she continued. "That I wouldn't get drawn into... this."

Tom stood and joined her, stopping just close enough that she could feel his presence without being crowded. "And now?"

"And now," Alice said quietly, "I don't think leaving fixes anything."

Tom's voice was low. "It fixes *you.*"

She turned to face him. "Does it?"

He hesitated. That was answer enough.

Alice stepped closer. The space between them closed without ceremony, without announcement. She could feel the heat of him now, the familiarity that had been waiting patiently for permission.

"This isn't just about the hall," she said. "It's about what happens if we don't go."

Tom's gaze dropped to her mouth, then lifted again deliberately. "It's also about what happens if we do."

Her pulse kicked. "Say it."

Tom's jaw tightened. "They'll provoke. They'll bait. They'll try to make you react so they can point at it later."

"And if I don't?"

"They'll push harder."

Alice reached out and rested her palm flat against his chest. Felt the steady beat beneath it. "You're not telling me anything I don't already know."

"I am," Tom said quietly. "I'm telling you I won't be able to stay restrained if they touch you."

The honesty of it sent a sharp, electric awareness through her.

"I don't want you to fight for me," she said.

Tom didn't look away. "I know."

"I want you beside me."

"Yes."

"And I want you choosing it," she added. "Not reacting."

Tom exhaled slowly. "That's harder."

"I know."

Ash cleared his throat with a small, indignant huff, reminding them he was still there.

Alice smiled faintly and stepped back. The moment loosened, but didn't disappear.

Later, they sat on the verandah wrapped in jackets, mugs cooling between their hands. The night air was damp, carrying the smell of impending rain that might never quite arrive.

Ash paced the length of the boards, stopped, paced again.

"He won't settle," Alice murmured.

Tom watched the pup, eyes narrowed slightly. "Neither will the town."

Alice's fingers tightened around her mug. "If we don't go tomorrow, they'll say we were afraid."

"And if we do?"

"They'll say we were arrogant."

Tom's mouth twitched. "Can't win."

Alice looked out into the dark. "I'm not trying to."

Silence settled, companionable and taut.

After a moment, Tom said, "If this goes wrong..."

Alice turned to him. "It won't."

"If it does," he continued, steady and deliberate, "I need you to know something."

She waited.

"I didn't come back to fix the past," Tom said. "I came back because you're here now."

The words landed harder than anything else that night.

Alice swallowed. "You brought a puppy."

Tom smiled faintly. "I hedge my bets."

She laughed softly, the sound brief but real.

Ash finally curled up at their feet, restless energy spent, nose tucked under his tail. The sight of him - small, stubborn, present - grounded her.

Alice leaned her shoulder against Tom's. "Tomorrow, we go."

Tom nodded. "Tomorrow, we go."

She closed her eyes briefly, letting the weight of the decision settle into something solid.

Because by morning, the town would have a room prepared.

And this time, Alice would walk into it knowing exactly what she was willing to lose - and what she wasn't.

Outside, Taravale held its breath.

Inside the house, the night stretched thin, waiting for daylight to decide what it would reveal.

CHAPTER EIGHTEEN

The hall smelled like polish and old dust.

That was the first thing Alice noticed - the deliberate cleanliness. Chairs stacked neatly along the walls, floor swept clean enough to erase footprints. Someone had prepared the space, not for an event, but for *control.*

Ash stiffened the moment they crossed the threshold.

His ears flattened, body lowering slightly, nose lifting to test the air. He didn't bark. He didn't hesitate.

He knew this place was wrong.

Tom closed the door behind them without comment. The sound echoed longer than it should have, reverberating off timber and stage boards that had heard generations of speeches, apologies, promises never kept.

A single light burned above the stage.

Maggie Rowley stood beneath it, hands clasped tight in front of her like she was holding herself together by force alone.

"I told you not to come," she said.

Alice didn't slow. "You told me not to look."

Maggie's mouth trembled. "It's not safe."

"It hasn't been for a long time," Alice replied.

Ash growled softly, a low vibration that filled the room without escalating it. Maggie flinched, eyes flicking down to the dog, then back up again.

"You've brought witnesses," Maggie said.

Alice stepped closer. "You already were one."

The light hummed overhead, harsh and unforgiving.

Maggie swallowed. "Daniel came here the night before he disappeared."

Tom's posture shifted instantly - not aggressive, but ready. "Who else was here?"

Maggie shook her head, panic rising. "I can't—"

A sound cut through her words.

A scrape. Slow. Deliberate.

Not from the front of the hall.

From the storage corridor behind the stage.

Ash barked once - sharp, sudden, warning.

Tom moved without thinking, stepping half a pace in front of Alice, shoulders squared, stance widening. His hand didn't clench, but Alice saw the restraint in it - the conscious choice *not* to act yet.

A man emerged from the shadows.

Middle-aged. Respectable. Dressed plainly enough to disappear into any crowd. The sort of face people trusted because it never showed too much of anything.

"Really," he said mildly. "We don't need an audience for this."

Maggie went pale. "I didn't call him."

"No," the man agreed. "But you always were predictable."

Alice felt something cold settle behind her ribs.

"You followed us," she said.

He smiled faintly. "You wanted to be followed."

Tom's voice was flat. "You should leave."

The man ignored him, eyes fixed on Alice. "You've made this unnecessarily difficult."

Alice met his gaze steadily. "You erased a man."

"He erased himself," the man replied calmly. "By insisting on stories that didn't belong to him."

"That's not how truth works," Alice said.

The man shrugged. "That's how towns work."

Ash growled again, louder this time, body angled protectively toward Alice.

The man's eyes flicked down to the dog. "Get control of that."

Tom's jaw tightened. "You're done giving instructions."

The man finally looked at Tom properly, assessing. Measuring. "You've always had a talent for overreacting."

Something dangerous flickered across Tom's face - anger sharpened by recognition.

Alice stepped forward before he could respond. "You were at the clean-up."

The man's smile thinned. "Careful."

"You signed off on what stayed buried," Alice continued. "And when Daniel found the discrepancy, you decided he didn't need to stay."

Silence dropped hard.

Not denial.

Calculation.

"You don't understand the consequences of what you're doing," the man said quietly.

Alice nodded. "I do. You're just not used to being included in them."

Tom moved then - not toward the man, but closer to Alice, presence unmistakable. "You don't get to manage this anymore."

The man's control slipped, just slightly. "You think exposing this makes you safe?"

"No," Alice said. "I think pretending nothing happened makes *you* desperate."

Maggie let out a shaky breath, eyes darting between them.

The man's voice hardened. "You're tearing open things that were settled."

Alice held his gaze. "They were buried. That's not the same thing."

Ash barked - loud, final - the sound echoing off the stage and down the corridor like a crack in glass.

For the first time, the man stepped back.

Not retreat.

Instinct.

"This isn't finished," he said.

Alice didn't blink. "No. It's exposed."

He turned and walked away, footsteps measured, controlled - the sound of someone already calculating damage.

Maggie sagged into a chair, shaking. "I'm sorry."

Alice knelt in front of her. "You don't get to apologise for surviving."

Tom stood watch at the door, eyes scanning the dark outside.

"They won't be quiet now," Maggie whispered.

Alice straightened. "They already weren't."

Outside, the air felt sharper, colder, like the night had teeth.

Ash pressed against Alice's leg, grounding, solid.

Tom rested a hand between her shoulders. "They've lost the room."

Alice nodded. "And people like him don't forgive that."

They stood there a moment longer, letting the truth settle where it couldn't be pushed back into shadow.

Because Taravale had just been forced to hear itself speak.

And it didn't like what it sounded like.

CHAPTER NINETEEN

The land went quiet before anyone spoke.

Not abruptly. Not dramatically. Just... deliberately.

The wind eased first, grass settling into itself as if it had been asked to behave. The magpies that had been calling from the far fence line fell silent one by one, their absence more noticeable than noise ever was. Even the flies thinned, drifting away from the clearing as though instinct recognised a boundary.

Ash stopped.

He had been moving ahead of them, nose down, tail level, mapping the ground with steady purpose. Now he froze mid-step, ears lifting, body going rigid in a way Alice had come to recognise.

This wasn't curiosity.

This was certainty.

Tom saw it too. He slowed, one hand lifting instinctively, palm out - not stopping Alice, just marking the moment.

"Here," he said quietly.

Alice didn't ask how he knew. She already did.

Her chest tightened, breath catching high and shallow, body responding before her mind could assemble language. She stepped forward anyway, boots sinking slightly into earth that felt heavier here, darker, damp in a way the rest of the paddock wasn't.

Ash let out a low sound - not a growl, not a bark - something unsettled and aching that vibrated through his chest. He glanced back at Alice once, eyes wide and questioning, then sat abruptly, tail tucked close to his body.

Alice knelt beside him without thinking, fingers curling into the fur at his neck.

"It's alright," she whispered.

The lie tasted bitter.

The clearing opened gradually, scrub thinning into a rough oval where the ground dipped unnaturally. Branches lay scattered across the space - not dumped, not piled - arranged just enough to soften what lay beneath.

The land hadn't hidden him.

It had tried to *hold* him.

Alice stopped breathing for a moment.

Daniel Bennett lay on his side, partially obscured by leaf litter and bark. His clothes were intact, though dirt-stained, one sleeve twisted awkwardly beneath him. His face was turned away, as if even in death he'd chosen not to look at what had been done.

He looked smaller than Alice expected.

Not diminished.

Just human.

"Oh," she whispered, the sound barely audible.

Tom removed his hat slowly, deliberately, pressing it against his chest as if he were standing in a church instead of a clearing that had learned too much.

Ash whimpered, rising to his feet and stepping forward once, then stopping himself. He didn't approach the body. He sat again, closer this time, eyes fixed, ears low.

"He knows," Alice murmured.

Tom nodded. "He understands enough."

The air smelled wrong now - faint but unmistakable. Not decay, not fully. The early, sickly sweetness of something that had been misplaced for too long.

Alice stood slowly, legs unsteady, and took a step closer.

"This wasn't meant to be permanent," she said.

Tom's voice was low. "No."

She crouched near Daniel's feet, careful not to touch anything, careful not to disturb what little dignity the land had preserved. Her eyes traced the details - the scuffed boots, the way one trouser leg had ridden up slightly, exposing pale skin already marked by insects.

"They moved him," she said.

Tom looked at her sharply. "What makes you think that?"

"The ground," Alice replied. "This isn't where he died. This is where he was... left."

The truth settled slowly between them.

They didn't speak again until the officers arrived.

There were no sirens.

No rushing.

Two utes came first, pulling up at a respectful distance. The officers stepped out quietly, movements economical, expressions sober. One of them - a woman Alice recognised from town, though not by name - removed her cap as she approached.

"We'll take it from here," she said gently.

Alice nodded, stepping back.

Ash didn't move.

The officer hesitated, then crouched slightly. "He can stay," she said. "As long as he doesn't interfere."

"He won't," Alice replied.

They worked carefully, methodically. Gloves pulled on. Photographs taken. Notes written in low voices that felt almost inappropriate in the stillness. Every movement seemed deliberate, as though the clearing itself demanded respect.

Alice stood and watched.

She didn't know why she needed to. Only that turning away felt like abandoning something unfinished.

Tom stayed close, not touching, just present - a steady line in her peripheral vision.

One of the officers lifted a branch away, revealing more of Daniel's torso. Alice's stomach clenched, grief rising sharp and sudden.

She hadn't known him.

Not properly.

But she knew what it meant to be erased.

A forensic specialist arrived next, movements precise, expression unreadable. She paused briefly when she saw Alice.

"Do you know him?"

Alice hesitated. "I knew of him."

The woman nodded. "That's enough."

When they rolled Daniel carefully onto the stretcher, the land seemed to exhale.

Not relief.

Acknowledgment.

Alice felt it in her knees, sudden and weak. The world tilted slightly, sound rushing back too fast - the rustle of leaves, the distant call of a bird that hadn't realised the moment had passed.

Tom's hand was at her elbow instantly, firm without pressure.

"I've got you," he murmured.

She didn't argue.

Ash stood then, stepping forward once, nose lifting as if memorising something important. He whined softly, tail low, then sat again as the stretcher was lifted.

When they carried Daniel away, the clearing felt wrong.

Not empty.

Displaced.

Alice stared at the disturbed ground where he'd lain, a hollow opening in her chest she hadn't expected.

"They'll say it's resolved now," she said quietly.

Tom nodded. "They always do."

Ash pressed against her leg, grounding, solid.

Alice swallowed. "But this doesn't fix anything."

"No," Tom agreed. "It changes things."

The officers packed up slowly, respectfully. One of them approached Alice again.

"We'll be in touch," she said. "There'll be questions."

Alice nodded. "I expect there will."

When they were gone, the paddock returned to itself gradually. Wind moved through grass again. Insects drifted back. Life resumed, not out of indifference, but necessity.

The land didn't follow them as they walked away.

It stayed.

Watching.

Remembering.

As Alice reached the fence line, she stopped and looked back one last time.

This place would never be ordinary again.

It had spoken.

And now it was waiting to see who would listen.

CHAPTER TWENTY

Alice couldn't wash the smell off.

She stood under the shower until the hot water thinned to lukewarm, then colder still, arms wrapped around herself as if holding her body together required conscious effort. She scrubbed her hands until the skin along her knuckles burned, then moved to her forearms, her neck, the place just below her collarbones where the air still felt wrong.

It wasn't a smell exactly. It was a presence.

Daniel Bennett was dead.

The fact sat inside her like a weight she hadn't decided where to set down yet.

When she finally turned the taps off, the silence rushed in too fast. The house made its small settling sounds - pipes ticking, timber contracting - noises she'd lived with all her life but which felt suddenly amplified, exposed.

She dried herself mechanically, dressed without looking in the mirror, then stood with her hand on the bathroom door longer than necessary.

Ash lay just outside it.

She hadn't asked him to stay there. He'd positioned himself deliberately, body stretched along the threshold like a living boundary. When the door opened, he lifted his head immediately, tail giving a single, solid thump before he settled again.

"You're not on duty," she murmured.

Ash didn't move.

She padded down the hallway barefoot, the floor cool beneath her feet. The closed room at the end of the hall felt heavier tonight, as if it were listening. She didn't stop. She didn't look.

Tom was in the kitchen.

Not sitting. Not pacing. Just standing at the bench, hands braced against the timber as though the house itself needed holding in place. A mug sat near his elbow, tea long gone cold.

"They'll come tomorrow," he said without turning.

Alice nodded. "I know."

The words felt inadequate, but there weren't better ones.

She crossed the room and sat at the table, elbows resting on the scarred surface, fingers lacing together too tightly. Her hands trembled slightly. She noticed and forced them still.

"I keep thinking," she said slowly, "about how ordinary today started."

Tom glanced at her then. "That's usually how it happens."

Ash padded in and placed his chin on her knee. She threaded her fingers through his fur automatically, grounding herself in the warmth and weight of him.

"They didn't panic," she said. "None of this feels panicked."

Tom pulled out the chair opposite her and sat. "It was managed."

"Yes." Her throat tightened. "That's what scares me."

Silence stretched between them - thick, not empty. The kind that demanded attention.

Outside, the wind picked up, rattling the loose section of guttering at the corner of the house. Ash's ears flicked, but he didn't lift his head.

Tom leaned back slightly. "This is the point where towns decide who they are."

Alice gave a short, humourless laugh. "I don't think Taravale wants to decide."

"No," Tom agreed. "It prefers inheritance."

The word landed hard.

Alice pushed back from the table and stood, pacing the length of the kitchen. Her body refused stillness. Stillness invited images she wasn't ready to carry - the shape of Daniel's body, the way the land had tried to soften him.

"I didn't know him," she said. "And I feel like I should."

Tom watched her carefully. "You knew what he represented."

"That shouldn't be enough to grieve," she snapped, then immediately softened. "Should it?"

Tom didn't flinch. "It often is."

She stopped pacing and pressed her palms flat against the bench. Her shoulders shook once, then stilled.

"I'm so tired," she said quietly.

Tom stood and moved closer - not touching, just near enough to be felt. "I know."

She turned suddenly, fiercely. "And I don't get to stop."

Tom met her gaze. "No."

Ash rose, momentarily unsettled by the surge of emotion, stepping between them before retreating once he realised neither was leaving.

Alice closed her eyes. "This isn't what I came back for."

Tom's voice was steady. "But it's what you found."

She swallowed. "What if this breaks something I can't fix?"

Tom hesitated. Then: "It already has."

Her breath caught.

"But broken isn't the same as gone," he added.

The words cracked something open.

Later, long after the lights were turned off, Alice lay awake in the dark. Ash pressed against her side, solid and warm. She could hear Tom moving in the next room - not restless, just there.

She didn't dream.

Taravale did not sleep.

It waited.

CHAPTER TWENTY-ONE

Alice lay in the dark with Ash pressed against her side, his warm weight steady and insistent, as if his body alone could keep the world from shifting under her. The old stone walls were cool even in late season, the kind of cool that crept quietly through skin and settled in bone.

From the next room, she could hear Tom moving.

Not restless.

Just there.

A floorboard creaked once - the familiar one near the hall - then the soft clink of a mug, a tap turned on and off, a quiet pause that felt like thought rather than hesitation. He wasn't trying to make noise. He wasn't trying to be silent either.

He was simply refusing to disappear.

Alice stared at the ceiling until the darkness began to lighten at the edges. Not dawn yet. Just the world loosening slightly, the sky thinning toward morning.

Ash sighed, long and deep, then lifted his head to listen.

So did Alice.

Nothing moved outside. No tyres on gravel. No distant voices. No gates creaking.

And still, the quiet didn't feel peaceful.

It felt staged - like the land itself was waiting for the next line to be delivered.

Alice shifted onto her back. The mattress sighed softly. Ash followed, sliding closer so his spine stayed pressed to her ribs. He wasn't sleeping properly either. His ears flicked at every change in the house's rhythm. He'd learned, quickly, that quiet could mean danger.

She rested her hand on his shoulder and felt him settle, just enough.

In the next room, Tom stopped moving.

Then, after a minute, his footsteps came down the hallway - slow, measured. He paused at her door.

"Are you awake?" he asked quietly.

"Yes," Alice said, and the word came out rougher than she meant.

There was a beat, as if he was deciding whether to step over a line.

Then the door opened a fraction and Tom appeared in the gap, the hall light behind him low and dim. He didn't fill the doorway. He didn't hover like a question.

He leaned one shoulder against the frame and looked at her as if checking she was still real.

"Sorry," he said. "Didn't mean to wake you."

"You didn't," Alice replied.

Ash gave a small, unimpressed huff, then sat up, ears pricked, gaze fixed on Tom like he was conducting his own assessment.

Tom's mouth twitched. "Alright, mate."

Ash did not move aside.

Alice didn't tell him to.

Tom's eyes flicked to the bedside table - the phone, the notebook, the small pile of paper that had become a second life she never asked for.

"You want tea?" he asked.

Alice nearly laughed. The idea of tea felt absurd - a domestic comfort in a house that now felt like evidence.

"No," she said. Then, after a breath, "Maybe."

Tom nodded once, the simple agreement of a man who didn't require her to choose perfectly.

He disappeared down the hallway again. Ash watched him go, then lay back down with a sigh that carried more emotion than it should have.

Alice sat up and swung her legs over the side of the bed. The floor was cold. The cold helped. It kept her present.

She pulled on a jumper and padded down the hall, moving quietly out of habit now - not to avoid waking anyone, but because the house had trained her to be careful long before she understood why.

In the kitchen, Tom stood at the bench with the kettle switched on. The light above the stove cast a soft, yellow pool across the room, leaving corners in shadow.

He hadn't sat down either.

He turned when he heard her.

His face looked older in this light. Not aged - stripped of softness. Like he'd spent the night holding something back by force.

Alice went to the other side of the bench and leaned her hip against it. Not touching him. Not distancing either. Just placing herself in the same room.

The kettle began to click as it heated.

Tom watched her for a moment, then said quietly, "You okay?"

Alice let the question hang.

She could have answered with competence. With defiance. With the version of herself that towns like Taravale expected - calm enough to swallow pain without spilling it.

Instead, she shook her head once.

"No," she said. "But I'm not... falling apart."

Tom's throat worked. He nodded. "Good."

The kettle clicked off. Tom poured water into two mugs, set one in front of her without ceremony, then leaned his forearms on the bench as if anchoring himself there.

Alice wrapped her hands around the mug. The warmth seeped into her palms. She didn't drink yet.

Ash padded in behind her and lay down at her feet, nose on his paws, eyes open. Always open.

Tom's gaze dropped to the dog. "He hasn't really slept."

"Neither have we," Alice said.

Tom didn't argue.

Silence gathered again - not empty, but dense with all the things neither of them wanted to say too quickly.

Alice stared at the steam rising from the mug and found herself thinking of Daniel Bennett's name, written in her own handwriting, neat and deliberate. Proof. Anchor. Refusal.

"He's not going to be erased," she said quietly.

Tom nodded. "Not now."

"And they'll hate that," Alice added.

Tom's jaw tightened. "Yes."

Alice looked up. "Not because they're sad. Not because they're shocked."

Tom met her gaze. "Because they didn't choose it."

She let out a slow breath. "Because it happened outside their control."

Tom's voice was low. "Because it makes them accountable."

The word settled heavy between them.

Alice stared down into the mug and finally took a sip. The tea was too hot. She welcomed the sting.

"There's a part of me," she said slowly, "that keeps waiting to be told I've done something wrong."

Tom went still.

Alice continued, voice steady now that she'd started. "Not wrong like... illegal. Wrong like... rude. Inconvenient. Disruptive. Like I've broken the rules of being polite in a place that doesn't deserve politeness."

Tom's eyes stayed on her. "You have."

Alice huffed a breath that was almost a laugh. "I know."

He leaned closer, just slightly. "You're not wrong, Alice. You're just not cooperating."

She swallowed. The tea tasted like nothing. Her throat tightened anyway.

"That's the thing," she said. "I'm not scared of what's true anymore. I'm scared of what they'll do to make everyone believe I'm the problem."

Tom's expression hardened. "That's already started."

"Yes," Alice said. "And I can feel it - like the town is arranging itself, quietly. Like furniture being moved in the dark."

Tom's mouth twitched, humourless. "They're good at that."

Alice's fingers tightened around the mug. "So what does it cost?"

The question came out softer than she intended.

It wasn't theoretical. It wasn't rhetorical.

It was the question at the centre of every choice she'd made since coming back.

Tom held her gaze.

Then he said, carefully, "It costs you comfort."

Alice waited.

"It costs you being liked," he continued. "It costs you being easy to talk about. It costs you being the kind of person they can put in a story without consequences."

Alice stared at him, the truth landing in slow increments.

"And it costs you sleep," Tom added quietly, eyes flicking toward the dark window. "Because you can't unsee what you've seen."

Ash shifted at her feet and let out a soft sound - a sigh, a breath, a tiny acknowledgement that felt like agreement.

Alice swallowed. "Does it cost you?"

Tom didn't answer immediately.

His gaze dropped to the bench, to his hands, to the place where he had learned to keep himself controlled.

Then he looked back up.

"Yes," he said simply.

Alice felt something in her chest loosen and ache at the same time.

"How?" she asked.

Tom's voice roughened slightly. "It costs me leaving you to it."

Alice went very still.

Tom continued, slower now. "It costs me pretending this isn't my fight. That I can keep my head down and watch you carry it because you're strong enough."

Alice couldn't find words. She just looked at him.

Tom exhaled, the sound quiet but heavy. "I'm not doing that anymore."

The sentence should have sounded like a vow. A dramatic line.

It didn't.

It sounded like the simple decision of a man who'd taken too long to choose the right side of his own life.

Alice set the mug down carefully.

Then, because her body needed something real, she walked around the bench and stopped in front of him.

Tom didn't move to meet her. He didn't reach.

He waited.

Permission, not possession.

Alice lifted her hand and rested it flat against his chest. Felt the steady beat beneath it, the warmth, the proof of him.

"You're here," she said.

Tom's voice was quiet. "Yes."

"And you'll still be here," she added, "when they start saying I'm unstable. When they start suggesting I'm... grieving wrong. When they start looking at me like I'm contagious."

Tom's mouth tightened. "Yes."

Alice searched his face. "And you won't try to fix it by making me quieter."

Something flickered in his eyes - respect, understanding, something like regret.

"I won't," Tom said. "I'll stand beside it. Not in front of you. Not behind you. Beside."

Alice breathed out slowly. The weight didn't lift - but it redistributed. It became bearable.

Ash stood and pressed his head against Alice's shin, then Tom's ankle, like he was ensuring the bond was sealed properly.

Tom glanced down. "He's a bloody negotiator."

Alice's mouth curved slightly. "He's a witness."

Tom looked up again. "They'll come for you socially now," he said. "Not with fists. Not with locks. With stories."

Alice nodded. "I know."

Tom's voice dropped. "And they'll come for me too."

Alice blinked. "Why?"

Tom met her gaze without flinching. "Because I'm still here."

The truth of it landed sharp.

Tom continued, steady and matter-of-fact. "They'll say I'm being manipulated. That I'm thinking with the wrong part of my body. That I'm doing this because I've got something to prove."

Alice felt heat rise - anger, but also something else.

"And are you?" she asked softly.

Tom's eyes held hers. "No."

A beat.

Then he added, with quiet honesty that made her throat tighten, "I'm doing it because I'm tired of being the man who watches."

Alice's fingers curled slightly against his shirt. She wanted to say something sharp, something clever, something that would keep the moment at a safe distance.

Instead, she stepped closer.

Tom's hands came to her waist, warm and certain, not pulling - steadying.

Their foreheads touched.

For a moment, the world narrowed to the simple truth of breath and skin and the sound of Ash settling back down at their feet.

"I don't want careful," Alice whispered.

Tom's mouth brushed her temple. "Neither."

He kissed her then - not hurried, not desperate. Grounding. Deliberate. The kind of kiss that didn't demand anything except presence.

Alice melted into it like her body had been holding itself rigid for days and finally found a place to lean.

When they broke apart, Tom didn't step away.

He didn't say the wrong thing.

He just stayed close, one hand at her back, as if reminding her she didn't have to brace alone.

Outside, a car passed on the road.

Neither of them flinched.

Ash's ears lifted. He watched. He listened. Then he rested his head again, satisfied.

Alice exhaled slowly. "Tomorrow will be worse," she said.

Tom nodded. "Yes."

"And we still go into town."

"Yes," Tom said again. "We go. We're seen. We don't apologise."

Alice stared out at the dark paddocks through the kitchen window. The land lay open and quiet, holding its shape, giving nothing away.

"I used to think being safe meant being liked," she said quietly.

Tom's voice came low and sure behind her. "Safety's not a feeling."

Alice nodded. "No."

She turned back to him, resolve settling like something physical in her chest.

"It's a decision," she finished.

Tom's eyes softened. "That's right."

A long silence followed - not awkward, not empty. The quiet of two people who had finally stopped negotiating with fear.

Tom lifted his mug, took a sip, then set it down as if it didn't matter.

Then he said, simply, "Come back to bed."

Alice hesitated. Not from doubt - from the strange unfamiliarity of being invited instead of managed.

"Okay," she said.

Ash stood first, as if approving the plan, and led the way down the hallway like he owned it.

In the bedroom, Alice slipped under the covers and felt her body finally register the possibility of rest. Ash curled against her side immediately, warm and solid.

A moment later, Tom lay down on the other side of the bed.

Not touching.

Just there.

The space between them felt deliberate - respect, not distance. Choice, not caution.

In the dark, Tom's hand found hers.

He didn't squeeze.

He didn't demand.

He simply held on, as if anchoring something quiet and stubborn into the future.

Alice stared at the ceiling and listened to the house settle, the old timber adjusting, the stone holding.

Outside, Taravale lay quiet.

Not innocent.

Not asleep.

Waiting.

But inside the farmhouse at Taravale, Alice finally closed her eyes - not because she believed the town would stop, but because she understood something she hadn't before:

Being seen was dangerous.

Being alone was worse.

And she was no longer alone.

CHAPTER TWENTY-TWO

They didn't rush it.

That was the mistake people made - thinking exposure looked like noise. Lights. Panic. Raised voices.

This was quieter.

The call went out midmorning. Formal. Unavoidable. By lunchtime, there were vehicles at the creek bend that didn't belong to Taravale, people walking the land with eyes that didn't soften at familiar names.

The town noticed.

Alice watched it happen from the verandah, mug warming her hands, Ash pressed against her leg like a second heartbeat. The road carried more traffic than usual - cars slowing, not to stare, but to confirm.

He   was   real.
He   existed.
He had been found.

Tom stood beside her, phone buzzing intermittently with messages he didn't answer.

"They won't like outsiders," he said.

"No," Alice replied. "They never do."

Ash barked once as a white vehicle passed the gate, then sat again, satisfied.

By afternoon, the story had shifted.

Not denial anymore. Reframing.

"Tragic."
"Unfortunate."
"No one could have known."

Alice heard it in fragments - through the shop window, in the careful phrasing of people who had practiced sympathy without responsibility.

Tom listened, jaw tight. "They're already distancing."

"Yes," Alice said. "They're deciding who they can afford to lose."

A car pulled into the drive just before dusk.

Claire stepped out slowly, face pale, eyes rimmed red. She stood there for a moment like she didn't trust her legs to hold her.

Alice went to her.

"They found him," Claire said, though it wasn't a question.

"Yes."

Claire nodded, absorbing it in pieces. "Was he—"

"No," Alice said gently. "He didn't suffer long."

Claire's shoulders sagged with relief sharp enough to hurt. She pressed a hand to her mouth and cried without sound.

Ash edged closer, resting his head against her knee. Claire startled, then crouched and wrapped her arms around him, fingers sinking into his fur.

"Thank you," she whispered to Alice. "For not letting him disappear."

Alice swallowed. "He mattered."

Claire nodded. "They're already saying things."

Alice's gaze hardened. "Let them."

Tom stepped closer. "They won't say his name more than they have to."

"They will now," Alice said. "It's written down. Logged. Witnessed."

Claire straightened slowly. "They're scared."

"Yes," Alice replied. "Because this time, the land didn't cooperate."

Night settled in, slow and heavy.

From the house, Alice could see lights moving at the edge of the paddock - torches, purposeful and unfamiliar. The land was being read by people who didn't belong to the story Taravale told itself.

Ash watched it all, alert but calm.

Tom rested a hand at the small of Alice's back. "You alright?"

She considered the question honestly. "No. But I'm clear."

He nodded. "That'll do."

Later, when the house was quiet again, Alice sat at the table and opened her notebook.

She wrote Daniel Bennett's name carefully. Below it, the date. The place.

Then, beneath that, another name.

The man in the photographs.

The pattern was visible now. Not speculation. Not paranoia.

Structure.

Ash lay at her feet, breathing slow and steady. Tom moved through the house, checking doors, grounding the night.

Outside, Taravale adjusted.

Not   gracefully. Not willingly.

But inevitably.

Because once the truth had a body, it couldn't be rewritten.

And this time, the land had witnesses.

CHAPTER TWENTY-THREE

By the next morning, the story had shifted again.

Not *what happened* - that was now fixed in place, anchored by vehicles that didn't belong to Taravale and people who didn't soften their language. That part couldn't be moved.

So the town moved the focus instead.

Alice felt it the moment she stepped outside.

The road was quieter, but not empty. Curtains twitched. A neighbour who usually waved turned his back and pretended to check a gate that didn't need checking.

She didn't wave either.

Inside the house, Tom read the local bulletin on his phone, jaw tightening with each line. "They're saying you stirred him up," he said finally.

Alice paused mid-step. "Daniel?"

"Yes." Tom met her eyes. "That you pushed him to keep digging. That you filled his head with stories."

Alice let out a short, incredulous breath. "I met him once."

"That won't matter," Tom said. "It sounds neat."

Ash trotted in from the yard and sat squarely in front of Alice, looking up at her like he was checking she was still there.

"They're building a version where I'm the catalyst," she said slowly. "Not the cause - just enough of one."

Tom nodded. "If they can make this about you, they don't have to talk about themselves."

A ute pulled up outside the gate.

This one *did* stop.

Alice and Tom exchanged a look, then stepped onto the verandah together. Ash planted himself between them, chest out, ears forward.

The man who climbed out was familiar - someone who had always been helpful in the vague, non-committal way that never required taking sides.

"Morning," he said, voice careful.

Alice didn't return the greeting. "What do you want?"

He shifted his weight. "People are asking questions."

"They should," Alice replied.

He cleared his throat. "There's talk that you've been... influencing things."

Tom stepped forward half a pace. "Say it properly."

The man's gaze flicked to Ash, then back up. "That you encouraged Daniel. That you led him into trouble."

Alice laughed once, sharp and humourless. "You erased him. Now you want to rewrite him."

The man's jaw tightened. "You don't need to make this worse."

Alice met his eyes. "I didn't make it."

Silence stretched. The man's shoulders slumped slightly, the confidence draining out of him.

"They're nervous," he said. "They think if this spreads—"

"It already has," Alice interrupted. "That's not my doing. That's consequence."

He hesitated, then tried again. "You could still help. Say you misunderstood. That you jumped to conclusions."

Tom's voice was flat. "You're asking her to lie."

"I'm asking her to keep the peace."

Alice stepped closer. "Peace built on disappearance isn't peace."

The man swallowed. "You're going to tear this place apart."

Alice held his gaze without blinking. "It was already broken."

He stood there a moment longer, then nodded once and turned back to his ute. He didn't look relieved - just tired.

As he drove away, Ash barked once, satisfied.

Tom exhaled slowly. "They've moved to blame."

"Yes," Alice said. "Which means they're out of denial."

Inside, the phone rang. Alice watched it for a moment before answering.

"Maggie," she said.

"They're saying awful things about you," Maggie whispered. "That you're unstable. That you've always been."

Alice's expression didn't change. "Did you hear any of them deny what happened?"

"No," Maggie admitted. "Just... why."

Alice nodded. "That's what they do."

After the call, she leaned against the bench, the weight of it finally landing. Not doubt - fatigue.

Tom stepped in front of her, hands resting lightly on her hips, grounding without trapping. "Hey."

She looked up at him. "They want me isolated."

"They won't get it."

She searched his face. "You're sure?"

Tom's thumb brushed her cheek, steady and sure. "I'm still here."

Ash barked softly and pressed his head against her knee, as if adding his own promise.

Alice rested her forehead briefly against Tom's chest, breathing him in. "Then let them talk."

Tom nodded. "We're not backing down."

Outside, Taravale rearranged its story again, trying to survive its own exposure.

Inside the house, Alice felt something settle - not fear, not anger.

Resolve.

Because if this was the price of refusing to disappear, she would pay it.

And she would not pay it alone.

CHAPTER TWENTY-FOUR

The email went out at 9:12 a.m.

Alice watched the sent notification appear and disappear, her cursor hovering for a moment longer than necessary, as if she could still pull it back.

She didn't.

There was no speech attached. No explanation. Just documentation - photographs, dates, names, locations. The pattern laid out cleanly enough that it didn't need interpretation.

Truth without commentary.

Tom leaned against the kitchen bench, arms crossed, watching her carefully. "That'll land."

"Yes," Alice said. "Exactly where it needs to."

Ash lay at her feet, chewing half-heartedly on a stick he'd stolen from the yard, eyes flicking up every time a car passed.

Within the hour, the first response came.

Not from town.

From outside it.

Alice read it once, then again, slower. "They want clarification."

Tom snorted. "That's polite for panic."

She smiled faintly. "They're asking the right questions."

The phone rang again. And again.

She let it.

By midday, Taravale was buzzing in a way it hadn't since the body was found. Not whispers this time - raised voices, fractured conversations, people trying to outrun something that had already reached them.

A ute screeched to a stop outside the gate.

Ash shot to his feet, barking sharp and fast.

The man from the hall climbed out, face flushed, control finally gone.

He didn't knock.

He walked straight up onto the verandah and pointed a finger at Alice. "You had no right."

Alice didn't move. "I had every right."

"You've dragged this into places it doesn't belong."

Tom stepped forward. "You dragged a body into a creek."

The man's jaw worked. "You don't understand how things work."

Alice tilted her head slightly. "I understand exactly how they worked."

He took a breath, trying to recalibrate. "You could still stop this. Clarify. Say it's being misinterpreted."

Alice's voice was calm. "I didn't interpret anything."

Ash growled low and steady, standing firm at her side.

The man's eyes flicked down to the dog, then back up. "You think this ends well for you?"

Alice met his gaze. "I think it ends."

Silence fell, thick and uncomfortable.

The man's shoulders slumped - not in defeat, but in realisation. He'd lost the space to manage this quietly.

"This town won't forgive you," he said.

Alice nodded once. "I'm not asking it to."

He stood there another moment, then turned away, walking back to his ute without another word. He didn't slam the door this time.

When he was gone, Alice exhaled slowly.

Tom rested his hand at the small of her back. "You alright?"

She nodded. "Yes."

She meant it.

That afternoon, the story broke properly.

Not as rumour. Not as grief.

As accountability.

Names appeared. Questions followed. The old fire was mentioned again - not as background, but as origin.

Taravale's neat explanations began to fracture under scrutiny.

Ash lay in the sun, finally relaxed enough to sleep properly, one paw twitching in a dream.

Alice watched him and felt something loosen in her chest.

This wasn't over.

But it was no longer contained.

And once truth left the valley, it didn't come back quietly.

CHAPTER TWENTY-FIVE

The house felt different once the noise faded.

Not quieter - clearer.

Alice noticed it in small ways: the way light pooled across the kitchen floor without feeling watched, the way her shoulders dropped when she realised she hadn't flinched at the sound of a car passing the gate.

Ash slept stretched out in the doorway, belly up, paws twitching as he chased something harmless through his dreams. For the first time in days, he looked like a puppy again.

Tom stood at the sink, sleeves rolled, washing dishes that didn't need washing. He did it slowly, deliberately, like he was resetting something inside himself.

Alice watched him for a moment before speaking. "You don't have to stay."

He didn't look at her. "I know."

"But you are."

"Yes."

That simple. That final.

She crossed the room and leaned against the bench beside him. Not touching yet. Just close enough to feel the heat of him.

"They're not going to stop talking," she said.

"No," Tom agreed. "But they're done controlling it."

Alice nodded. "I don't know what Taravale looks like after this."

Tom shut off the tap and turned to face her. "It'll look like itself. Just more honest."

She studied his face - the lines she knew, the steadiness she trusted. "And us?"

He didn't hesitate. "That depends on what you want."

The weight of the question settled between them.

Alice thought of the shed door closing. The phone in the mud. The body by the creek. And the way Tom had never stepped back once he came forward.

"I want this," she said quietly. "Not hiding. Not careful. Not half-present."

Tom reached for her then, hands warm and certain at her waist. "Good."

The kiss wasn't desperate or defiant. It was slow, grounding, the kind that made space instead of urgency. Alice melted into it, fingers curling into his shirt like she was anchoring herself.

Ash stirred and let out a small huff, unimpressed by the interruption to his sleep.

Tom smiled against her mouth. "He's judging us."

"He'll get over it."

They laughed softly - the sound surprising them both.

Later, they sat on the verandah as dusk settled, shoulder to shoulder, the land stretching out before them in long, familiar lines. The paddocks didn't look healed. They didn't look broken either.

They just were.

"I used to think staying meant accepting things," Alice said.

Tom glanced at her. "And now?"

"Now I think it means deciding what doesn't get to stay."

Tom nodded. "That sounds right."

Ash padded out and settled at their feet, leaning into Alice's leg, content and solid.

Alice rested her hand on his head and felt the simple truth of it settle fully.

The land had revealed what it needed to.

What came next wouldn't be quiet - but it would be chosen.

CHAPTER TWENTY-SIX

Taravale didn't fracture all at once.

It adjusted.

Alice saw it in the days that followed - not in apologies or admissions, but in movement. People left town earlier than planned. Others stayed indoors longer. Conversations changed shape, thinning at the edges where certainty used to sit.

Names stopped being spoken casually.

The creek bend was taped off, then walked, then walked again by people who didn't soften their steps out of habit. Vehicles came and went. Questions were asked without deference. Answers were written down exactly as given, without being tidied afterward.

The land didn't care.

It held its lines the way it always had - fences still crooked where they'd always been, paddocks still brittle underfoot, gumtrees shedding bark in long, pale ribbons that caught the light and fell without drama.

Alice moved through her days deliberately.

She spoke when asked. She corrected what was wrong. She didn't volunteer comfort.

Claire stayed in town longer than she'd planned. Long enough to attend the formal identification. Long enough to say Daniel's name out loud in places it had been avoided.

"Thank you," she said again, the morning she left. "For not letting him be nothing."

Alice shook her head. "He never was."

Ash sat at their feet as they talked, head resting on Alice's boot, eyes half-closed. He'd grown in the last week - not physically, but in the way dogs did when the world asked something of them and they answered.

Tom watched it all quietly.

He didn't insert himself. Didn't manage the narrative. He fixed fences where they needed fixing. Walked the boundary lines again. Let the land do what it had always done best - tell the truth slowly, without embellishment.

One afternoon, Alice followed him out to the far paddock, Ash racing ahead, ears flapping wildly as he chased a phantom only he could see.

"This was where it started," Alice said, stopping beside him.

Tom nodded. "And where it changes."

She looked out across the grass, thin and sun-bleached, the soil cracked in places where water had never quite returned after the fire years ago. "I don't think it ever really goes back."

Tom met her gaze. "No. But it doesn't have to."

They stood there together, no urgency now, no need to decide everything at once.

Later, as evening settled, Alice sat at the kitchen table with her notebook open one last time. She added a final entry - not a name, not a date.

A decision.

She closed the book and slid it into the drawer.

Ash curled up beneath the table, sighing deeply as he dropped into sleep. Tom moved through the house behind her, familiar and unhurried, a presence that no longer felt temporary.

Outside, Taravale quietened again - not the old quiet of omission, but something closer to acceptance. Not healed. Not absolved.

Aware.

Alice stepped out onto the verandah as the last light faded, the land stretching away from her in long, unbroken lines.

She wasn't finished with it.

But she wasn't alone in it either.

And for the first time since she'd come back, the land didn't feel like it was asking her to carry anything it couldn't hold itself.

CHAPTER TWENTY-SEVEN

By morning, everyone knew.

Not the details. Not the truth.

But the shape of it.

Alice felt it the moment she stepped into town - the way conversations stalled when she passed, the way faces turned just slightly away. The bakery bell rang too loudly when she entered, the sound lingering a fraction longer than it should have. A woman mid-sentence stopped speaking altogether, eyes dropping to the counter like she'd been caught doing something wrong.

Ash walked close, shoulder brushing Alice's leg, head high. He wasn't anxious. He was attentive - cataloguing changes, mapping the shift in tone the way dogs did instinctively.

The first thing Alice noticed wasn't hostility.

It was subtraction.

The woman who used to wave from her kitchen window didn't look up this time. The man who once stopped her to talk fences crossed the road before she reached him. A neighbour who'd borrowed sugar from her mother for years pretended to be absorbed in checking tyre pressure that didn't need checking.

Nothing dramatic. Nothing that could be confronted.

Just absence.

"They've decided," Alice murmured.

Ash flicked an ear but kept walking.

At the bakery, the girl behind the counter smiled too brightly. Too carefully.

"What can I get you?"

Alice ordered the same bread she always did.

The girl rang it up quickly, eyes fixed on the register. Her fingers shook slightly when she handed over the change.

"Busy?" Alice asked, not unkindly.

The girl swallowed. "People are... talking."

Alice nodded. "About Daniel?"

A pause - brief, loaded.

"About you," the girl said quietly.

That landed harder.

Outside, the air felt tighter, like the town had drawn an invisible boundary and was waiting to see whether Alice would step outside it or apologise herself back in.

She did neither.

She walked on.

At the post office, the clerk slid Alice's mail across the counter without meeting her gaze. Her voice was low, cautious. "You should take a break."

Alice stilled. "From what?"

"All of this." A small, apologetic shrug. "Let it settle."

Alice looked at her steadily. "People don't settle when they've done nothing wrong."

The clerk flushed. "I just meant—"

"I know what you meant," Alice said evenly.

Outside, Maggie Rowley stood near the noticeboard, hands clasped tight in front of her. She looked smaller than Alice remembered - shoulders rounded inward, like she was bracing for impact.

"They came by last night," Maggie said without preamble.

Alice's pulse ticked up. "Who?"

"You know who." Maggie swallowed. "They didn't threaten me. That's what scared me."

Ash sat at Alice's feet, eyes fixed on Maggie's face.

"What did they say?" Alice asked.

Maggie laughed once, brittle. "That they were worried about you. That grief does strange things to people. That I should be careful not to get caught up in someone else's... spiral."

The anger arrived cold and precise.

"They're trying to isolate you," Alice said.

"They're trying to make me doubt you," Maggie whispered.

Alice stepped closer, voice steady. "Do you?"

Maggie hesitated. Then shook her head. "No."

Relief flickered - fragile, brief.

"But I don't know how long I can keep saying that out loud," Maggie added.

That was the point.

They didn't need Alice silenced.

They needed her unsupported.

Ash stood and pressed against Alice's leg, grounding, solid.

"They're testing who folds," Alice said quietly. "And who disappears quietly enough that no one notices."

Maggie's eyes filled. "I don't want to disappear."

"Then don't," Alice said. "But don't expect them to make it easy."

They walked on.

At the shop, Linda greeted her too brightly. "Such a terrible thing."

Alice nodded. "It didn't happen in isolation."

Linda's smile wavered. "Well. It's finished now."

Alice met her eyes steadily. "Is it?"

Linda looked away first.

Ash stopped abruptly near the hall steps and sat, staring at the closed doors.

Alice followed his gaze.

"They're remembering," she murmured.

The hall had always been where Taravale laundered its conscience - meetings that went nowhere, apologies that softened responsibility. Now it stood silent, doors shut, waiting to be reopened whether it liked it or not.

Alice rested a hand on Ash's head. "Not today."

They turned back toward the ute.

Behind them, Taravale shifted uncomfortably.

Memory, once stirred, didn't return neatly to silence.

The test came that afternoon.

Not dramatic. Not threatening.

Official.

A car Alice didn't recognise pulled up at the gate as she returned home. Ash barked once, sharp and alert, then went still.

Two people stepped out. One man. One woman. Dressed neutrally enough to pass anywhere without being remembered.

"Ms Gordon?" the woman asked.

"Yes."

"We're just checking in," the man said smoothly. "Making sure you're alright."

Alice didn't invite them onto the verandah.

"I'm fine," she said.

The woman smiled sympathetically. "A lot has happened very quickly. Sometimes people benefit from... support."

Ash growled low in his chest.

The man glanced down. "We'd appreciate if you kept him calm."

Alice's gaze hardened. "He is calm."

A beat.

"We've had concerns raised," the woman continued. "About your wellbeing. About whether the stress of recent events may be affecting your perception."

There it was.

Alice didn't react. Didn't argue.

She smiled - small, controlled.

"Who raised them?" she asked.

The woman hesitated. Just long enough.

"That's not how this works," the man said.

Alice nodded. "Then this isn't how it ends."

Silence stretched.

"We're not accusing you of anything," the woman said quickly.

"No," Alice agreed. "You're positioning me."

The man straightened slightly. "You need to understand how serious this is."

Alice stepped forward half a pace. Ash stood with her, shoulder squared.

"I understand exactly how serious it is," Alice said. "Which is why this conversation ends now."

The woman's smile finally faltered. "You're being uncooperative."

Alice held her gaze. "I'm being visible."

A long moment passed.

Finally, the man nodded. "We'll be in touch."

Alice watched them leave without moving.

When the car disappeared down the road, she exhaled slowly.

Ash sat and leaned against her leg, solid and unshakeable.

"That's it," Alice murmured. "That was the line."

The town had tried silence. Then concern. Then erasure. Now credibility.

And it had failed.

Alice rested her hand on Ash's head and looked out across Taravale - the land wide, patient, incapable of lying no matter how carefully people tried to speak over it.

"They won't stop," she said quietly.

Ash's tail thumped once.

"No," she agreed. "But neither will I."

EPILOGUE

The land changed first.

Not dramatically. Not in a way anyone could point to and say *this is where it happened.* But Alice noticed it all the same - the way the paddocks seemed to breathe again, the way the wind moved through the grass without catching, without sounding like warning.

Morning came cool and pale, frost thin along the fence lines. Gumtrees shed bark in long ribbons that curled at her feet as she walked, the sound sharp and clean in the air. Ash trotted ahead of her, nose low, reading the ground like a story written only for him.

Taravale had not apologised.

It never would.

What it had done instead was adjust - the way towns always did when forced to carry something they'd tried to bury. Conversations resumed, but more carefully now. Names were spoken with pauses around them. Some people crossed the road when they saw Alice coming. Others nodded, stiff but deliberate, as if acknowledging a line that had been drawn and held.

The house felt different too.

Not lighter - truer.

Rooms no longer seemed to wait for explanation. They simply existed, contradictions intact. The closed room remained closed, but it no longer felt like a threat. It was just a room again - one part of a larger structure that had stopped trying to decide who was allowed inside.

Alice learned the house's rhythms again, not as a child and not as a visitor, but as someone who stayed long enough for patterns to matter. She stopped bracing herself for what might be said and started listening to what wasn't.

The case moved forward in the way cases did - incrementally, without ceremony. Statements were taken. Documents surfaced. Questions were asked that could no longer be redirected without effort. Daniel Bennett's name appeared in print more than once this time, no longer framed as inconvenience or rumour.

Some families closed ranks.

Others didn't.

That was the part no one talked about - the small fractures, the quiet realignments. Who sat beside whom at the pub. Who stopped attending committee meetings. Who began leaving town earlier than they'd planned.

Taravale remembered.

Not kindly. Not cleanly. But it remembered.

One afternoon, Alice stood at the fence line with Tom, boots muddy, the air warm enough to suggest summer hadn't quite finished with them yet. Ash lay stretched between them, head on his paws, eyes half-closed but alert all the same.

"I used to think the land needed protecting," Alice said.

Tom glanced at her. "From people?"

"From forgetting," she replied. "Turns out it was people who needed reminding."

Tom smiled faintly at that.

They didn't talk about leaving.

They didn't talk about staying.

Those conversations felt premature - like naming something before it had decided what shape it wanted to take.

Instead, they stood together and watched the paddocks shift colour as the light changed, watched Ash lift his head suddenly at a sound only he could hear.

Later, when the sun dipped and the air cooled, Alice locked the doors out of habit.

Then stopped.

She unlocked one again.

Not because she was reckless.

Because she understood the difference now - between fear and vigilance, between being guarded and being erased.

Ash settled near the threshold, body angled toward the dark, content in his role as witness.

Inside, the house held the warmth of the day.

Outside, the land stretched wide and patient, bearing no allegiance except to what endured.

Taravale had tried to decide what would be remembered.

It hadn't succeeded.

Because memory, once claimed, did not belong to those who wished it quiet.

And Alice - no longer returning, no longer passing through - understood something she hadn't when she first came back:

The land did not keep secrets.

It waited.

And when the time came, it gave them back.

What the Land Returns comes next.

ABOUT THE AUTHOR

Emily Fraser writes rural romantic suspense set in Australia, where landscape is not a backdrop but a force - shaping lives, loyalties, and the choices people make when silence feels safer than truth.

Her Taravale Series explores land, memory, consequence, and the cost of speaking up in small communities, telling stories where love is tested not by the absence of feeling, but by the courage to act when staying quiet would be easier.

What the Land Keeps introduced readers to Taravale.
What the Land Leaves deepened the story, shifting from inheritance to consequence.
What the Land Reveals brings the series to its most dangerous reckoning yet.

Emily lives and works on the land she writes about, where days are shaped by weather, work, and the long memory of place.